KEEPING DOWNWIND

Lone Huntress Series
Book Three

Andrew Miller

AP Miller Productions

Book List

Books written by Andrew Miller
Lone Huntress Series (Scifi):
Lone Huntress
Bems and Bugs
Paranormal Stand Alone:
Unique
Middle-Grade Stand Alone
Michael Williams Lives in Space
Children's Picture Books:
Elliot Finds a Home Series
Aura Shemen

Copyright © 2024 by Andrew Miller

All rights reserved.

No part of this publication may be reproduced, distributed, or transmitted in any form or by any means, including photocopying, recording, or other electronic or mechanical methods, without the prior written permission of the publisher, except as permitted by U.S. copyright law. For permission requests, contact Andrew Miller archone89144@yahoo.com.

The story, all names, characters, and incidents portrayed in this production are fictitious. No identification with actual persons (living or deceased), places, buildings, and products is intended or should be inferred.

Book Cover by TMT Book Cover Designs

Illustrations by TMT Book Cover Designs

Formatting by S.A Soule of Creativity Coaching.

First Edition 2024

Excerpt

"The Federation investigation team put their ship on hover above the ocean, and sent down a probe on a cable. It went down... oh, about three, maybe four kilometers... and then a giant tentacle grabbed it."

Lisa had munched on noodles and listened with interest, despite the headache from her injuries. "It shook the probe like a rattle," Patrick had continued, while she ate. "Then it tied the cable in knots... and then..." Patrick paused, frowning at the recollection. "And then it gave the entire thing a sharp *yank*." He snorted, shaking his head in wry amusement. "Probably would have pulled the ship under, if they hadn't detached the cable."

"So what happened to the probe?" Lisa had asked.

"A couple of smaller Octopussies returned it. Dumped it on the docks like they were tossing out garbage."

"So that's what convinced everyone the Octopussies were sapient," Lisa mused.

"Well, that and the knots in the line. Perfect bowline on a bight."

Dedication

*To my Samuel. Twelve years was not enough.
And to Bob, for reminding us all of the magnificent brilliance of
octopuses. If they lived after mating, what cultures and societies might
they craft, below the waves?*

KEEPING DOWNWIND

Chapter 1

The fox crept through the woods, attempting to conceal herself from her stalker, but the Huntress had her scent. Soft padded feet tiptoed with a slow, measured gait, carefully lowering her weight onto the damp fallen leaves and rich loamy soil. Red fur did its best to blend in against the brown shades of tree bark as the hunted vixen sought to evade her predator.

She never saw it coming. Like countless prey before her, she was largely focused on threats coming from the four cardinal directions. It hadn't occurred to her to look up, or down. The fox looked over her shoulder to check if her trail was being followed, then ahead to see if she'd been cut off – then gave a single short yelp as a much larger, stronger, and deadlier creature came down from above, leaving its perch in the branches of the closest tree to seize the fox with two powerful limbs. The predator's jaws parted wide, then clamped down onto the captured vixen's throat.

The fox gasped, stiffened as if paralyzed, feeling the predator's teeth through her fur. Then she practically melted, leaning back into her attacker's chest with a submissive mewling. "Ahh... you got me..." Jenny moaned, one hand sliding over one of her captor's powerful limbs in a tender caress.

Lisa declined to answer, at least with words, as she continued to nibble and nuzzle at the Furcadian's throat. Jenny began to undulate, her shapely transhuman body slowly writhing against her amazonian friend, while she began to make soft growling noises of utter delight.

Finally Lisa came up for air, murmuring softly, "You did a little better this time." She relaxed her hold enough for Jenny to pull free or turn to face her if she so chose.

Jenny opted to do neither, instead continuing to grind her soft furred tail and buttocks against Lisa as if performing a lap dance, despite standing upright. "I still don't get it," she whined, her tone an exaggerated pout to further titillate her friend. "How do you keep finding me?"

Lisa grinned as she teased the vixen. "You haven't figured it out yet?" she purred, her deep, husky voice taking on a suggestive quality that would have shocked those who had only met her in a professional capacity.

"Tell me," Jenny whined, pouting like a spoiled little girl even as she ground herself against her muscular playmate.

Lisa chuckled, unable to resist. "It's your perfume, silly," she pointed out. "The whole *point* of perfume is to attract with your scent. It's not exactly something you want to wear if you're trying to avoid getting caught."

Jenny made a face, her long muzzled features twisting with self-disgust at the belated realization. "Oh, nuts." Nonetheless she continued to grind against her companion, almost unconsciously maintaining the seductive behavior. "I didn't even think I'd put that much on," she groused.

"For most people, maybe," Lisa conceded, before nuzzling at Jenny's throat again. She inhaled, taking a long, deep whiff of the scent arising from fur on the fox's neck, before shuddering with a sensuous thrill. "Mmmm... but I'm Gaian. My nose is more sensitive than most people's. Even a Furry's."

Jenny moaned more heatedly, her hands coming up to grip at Lisa's forearms. She didn't appear to be able to tell the difference between the organic limb and the prosthetic by touch alone. Then again, Lisa's cybernetic limb was covered in synthetic flesh and certainly looked like a mirror image of its counterpart to a casual glance. "I suppose your eyes are better than mine, too?" the vixen playfully pouted.

"Not really," Lisa confessed. "Gaian eyes are adapted for low light and close range..." She hesitated, biting her lip before admitting the truth. "The fact is, I'm considered nearsighted by most people's standards. I can see really well up close, but... well, my helmet's got custom visual compensation software."

Jenny sniffed, dropping the pretense of a bratty pout. "And here I thought you were more evolved, what with the forced natural selection and all," she ruminated.

"Evolution just means adaptation to conditions," her taller, muscular, fur-less friend pointed out. "Gaians are adapted to surviving in a big, dark forest." She kissed Jenny's throat again, before adding, "besides, you're Furcadian. You guys left natural selection behind when you colonized this planet."

Jenny giggled and squirmed, finally twisting around to face Lisa. "Why settle for natural when you can be perfection?" she crooned coyly, as her hands began to slide over the taller woman's powerful torso.

"Mmm. Fair point," Lisa agreed, her broad grin causing her face to begin to ache slightly. *I never smiled this much in my life, before I came here.* Her arms tightened their hold, pulling

Jenny closer. "Anyway, I caught you again. We agreed, best two out of three."

Jenny tilted her head in, planting a soft smooch against Lisa's chest, before pulling back to ask, "seriously, though. How am I supposed to avoid you tracking my scent, next time?"

Lisa shrugged slightly; the movement caused Jenny to be pulled in closer yet, and the vixen wriggled appreciatively against that hefty bosom. "You just have to keep downwind," Lisa answered.

"Yeah?" Jenny gave that chest another kiss, her hands doing interesting things to a pair of buttocks thick and rounded with muscle beneath the fabric of Lisa's pants. "What does that even mean? Downwind, upwind, I don't get it."

Lisa sighed heavily as she considered how to explain it. "When the wind travels from one place to another," she replied slowly, attempting to coach it in terms that her decidedly urban friend would understand, "it carries scent along with it. So it's like... a river. Being upstream or downstream. If you're downwind, the wind carries my scent to you, but your scent gets carried further down."

Jenny harrumphed, before asking the obvious question. "So what happens if the wind changes?"

Lisa shrugged. "It happens. You can't stop it, you just try to deal with it." She sighed again, this time from pleasure at Jenny's exquisite caresses. "Sometimes hunting – or escaping the hunter – is luck as much as skill."

Jenny made a grumbling noise, then sighed. "Right. Well, a deal's a deal. Though I'm telling you, it's not going to be that hard."

"You know how I feel about... well..." Lisa released Jenny, taking a step backwards and waving her hand at herself. A broad gesture to indicate the entirety of her appearance. "...This."

"You know how the rest of us feel about it," Jenny countered, reaching out to seize that hand in her own. "Just leave yourself in my oh so capable paws," she grinned, her fangs gleaming as she began to walk towards the edge of the orchard, "and I'll have every stud, buck, and bull drooling and fighting over you."

Lisa felt her cheeks flush crimson as she gulped, but nodded silently and allowed the shorter, slimmer, far more socially adept woman to lead her by the hand. But internally she felt her self-loathing once again beginning to uncoil and slither about, spreading rancid slime through her thoughts with whispered little suggestions and toxic innuendo. *Bull. Including one particular bull.*

Lisa had been adjusting rather nicely to Furcadian culture, once she'd gotten past the initial shock that came from being confronted with their polyamorous lifestyles and casual approach to sexuality. She had allowed herself to enjoy not one, but two – *two!* – lovers. Harvey was a diminutive sex machine that left her purring contentedly and feeling almost meek whenever he turned his bucktoothed grin upon her, while Jenny was a sensual sapphic thrill who had proven herself capable of achieving the seemingly impossible: making Lisa (occasionally) forget to feel like a hulking, hideously deformed freak covered in scars and with a missing limb. Every now and then Jenny succeeded in making her feel like the gorgeous statuesque goddess her friends all insisted that she was, pushing the impostor syndrome at bay for tantalizingly brief moments.

But someone else wanted to be her third pleasure partner while she remained on this planet, and Lisa hated herself for having not dared to take the first step yet. All the more so because Brutus was her masculine counterpart; one of the few people Lisa knew who stood taller than she did, yet oh so gentle, even shy. He'd told her pointedly that he would wait for her to make the first move, to put her at her ease. No pressure. *All the pressure.* Damn it. *Why can't I just let myself enjoy myself with my friends?*

Lisa did her level best to maintain her cheerful disposition for the benefit of her sweet vulpine friend, even as her self-loathing continued to spread its pollution over her internal thoughts. *Just like usual.*

Chapter 2

Lisa frowned thoughtfully as she regarded the image before her. On the one hand, an objective critique of her appearance, within this particular setting, seemed entirely appropriate. The shorts hugging her rear and the tops of her thighs were as appropriate for the exercise room as the midriff baring top. In such a setting her bared skin – and with it the scars showing as lighter colored streaks and slight ridges of tissue over the thick musculature of her limbs – shouldn't make her feel embarrassed. Particularly given her awareness that the figure stepping into the room on cloven hooves the size of dinner plates was thoroughly captivated by her appearance.

At least, if he were telling the truth about his attraction to her.

Stop that. He's honest and I know it. "Good afternoon, Brutus," she murmured without so much as turning her head.

Brutus' bovine features split in an amused grin. "You know, that always seems impressive to new students," he reflected, glancing from her to the mirror running the length of the wall. And two other walls for good measure.

"I guess that's why they put mirrored walls in training halls," she suggested, and her shoulders bunched up until they seemed like a pair of boulders with her shrug. Beneath them, a pair of similarly sized mounds jiggled; Lisa tried to suppress the embarrassment. But the mirrors were making it nigh impossible to escape her own appearance.

"I think it's more about letting the teacher see what every student's doing," Brutus murmured in a gentle tone. As always, his massive size – even larger than her own! – belied his gentle, charitable nature. "And so students can see themselves from multiple angles," he added.

"Don't I know it," Lisa muttered, glancing to the side. With three walls embossed with mirrors, she could not only behold her garishly over-muscled chest and arms, but also a rump that could only be described as amazonian. The afternoon sunlight shining through the full length windows of the fourth wall provided ample illumination for such inspection.

Stop it. He likes how my butt looks. She took a deep breath, then turned to face him. *Deep breaths.* "So why don't they just use cameras?" she wondered, lifting up her hands to inspect the thickly padded gloves she'd donned in preparation for their workout.

"Low tech's cheaper," Brutus replied, lifting his own gloved hands to clasp before him in a respectful salute, before sinking into a fighting stance.

Well, there was no arguing with that. Particularly not when their workout session was about to begin. Brutus' desire to train against her was practically masochistic; for her part the prospect of working with a larger sparring partner was too rare and valuable an opportunity to pass up. She shifted into her own stance and began to flow towards him like a river unleashed from a broken dam.

Brutus was large, strong, and well trained in basic techniques for his own fighting style, but Lisa had been helping him to improve in the one area where he lacked. Namely, his hesitancy. Like most people, the brutish bovine possessed an instinctive reluctance to inflict pain and harm upon other living things, and overcoming that reluctance was as much a part of the mental training as overcoming the fear that inevitably accompanied mortal danger.

Granted, learning to overcome both required near-traumatic levels of conditioning, of repeated exposure to stressful situations until one became comfortable with functioning through pants-wetting terror. Until one became comfortable with performing the physical actions necessary to harm another. Was it merely a desire to sacrifice of oneself for the sake of protecting others that drove a person to learn such things?

Not even remotely.

There it is. Lisa felt it beginning inside of her, that sensation that was still one of her favorite things in life. The adrenaline was coursing through her body, endorphins were flowing, as she achieved her fight-or-flight mode – and with it, the unmistakable high that was one of the highlights of her life as a professional dealer in violence. Even though they'd agreed to limit themselves to light contact – at her insistence – every blow that landed left a painful sting, or worse. Each painful impact followed by a euphoric wave, as she gave to, and received from, her sparring partner. Her *partner*. Her collaborator and teammate in this act of mutual self-improvement.

Brutus was definitely receiving the worst of it, though his improvement was unmistakable. The first time they'd sparred he had braced himself before each heavy swing of his limbs, his body tense and slowed by his nervous hesitancy. But that had been months ago, and he'd learned to relax his muscles, to flow more smoothly and deliver combinations rather than brief little spurts of one or two strikes at a time. He was as gentle and compassionate as ever, but he was learning to subconsciously steel himself when necessary.

But as much as Brutus had improved, Lisa still had far more practical experience with far more stressful situations than a bout of light sparring. Her next combination began with a lead hand punch to his midsection, followed by a lunging, diving, open handed punch aimed *behind* his lead foot. *Hoof. Whatever.* The bull gave a startled grunt as he found himself on the receiving end of a single leg takedown, before landing heavily on his back.

Before he could think to react, Lisa had swarmed over him with that same liquid flow to her movements, straddling her fallen partner. Normally she didn't bother with groundwork; she was accustomed to fighting in armor, while wielding weapons capable of unleashing death and devastation from a distance, and under such conditions anyone on the ground was as good as dead. But grappling on the ground still had its uses, under certain limited conditions, and she wasn't completely unfamiliar with it.

Her attempts to achieve a stranglehold were complicated by her wariness of his horns. One of the reasons why ground based grappling was generally regarded as an esoteric area with limited applications was the prevalence of weaponry. Simply put, sharp and pointy things (such as the two sharp pointy things jutting out of Brutus' skull, just above his temples) made sport-viable techniques extremely ill-advised, under non-sport conditions. Lisa was forced to lean back repeatedly, sinking her weight backwards onto her rear as she sought to avoid the tips of those horns.

Then her movements slowed to a halt.

Brutus also ceased his struggles, as he stared up at her

with a somewhat chagrined expression plastered across his bestial features. Her own cheeks flushed scarlet as she returned his gaze.

She bit her lip, felt her blush deepen and spread. A physiological response not unlike the one she was reacting to. Brutus looked utterly mortified, like a child (or a calf) who had been caught with a hand (or a hoof) in the cookie jar.

Then she flinched and yelped, "is it still growing?"

Brutus winced, but managed to groan a mortified response. "I *am* a bull, you know," he pointed out, despite his embarrassment.

Lisa stared down at him for a few moments longer. Long enough to confirm that yes, he did indeed still have further to go before achieving full tumescence. At which point she leapt off him, scrambling to her feet and turning away to stare at the floor. She could feel her limbs shaking, and not from the adrenaline surge they'd been enjoying prior to his physical reaction.

She heard him grunting as he rolled over and struggle to a standing position, saw his movements in the mirror. She did not look at him, as her personal discomfort and her guilt flowed and surged and coiled together inside of her. *Damn it. I made everything worse.*

Then Brutus said the worst possible thing he could have, under the circumstances. "I'm sorry," he rumbled softly, sounding utterly ashamed of himself.

Lisa felt her hands clenching into fists, until the knuckles of her organic limb began to pop, until she feared her prosthetic limb's fingers might be damaged by the strain. "Don't!" she snapped viciously, before hastily amending it. "Don't... apologize. That makes it worse."

"I'm so- I mean, if I upset you..." Brutus stammered,

looming behind her, his hands held out in a supplicating gesture.

"I'm upsetting myself," she seethed, through clenched teeth. "You're not doing anything wrong. I'm the one upsetting myself."

Brutus shut his mouth and said nothing, waiting on her to say more.

Deep breaths. She gulped once, twice, three times, exhaling each lungful of air with a heavy rush. Then she reiterated, "I'm upsetting myself." Another deep breath, and she forced herself to articulate the truth. "I'm upset... because... I really, really like you," she groaned, shutting her eyes tightly and shaking her head. "But I'm having trouble getting past my... my issues."

Lisa took another deep breath. Then another, as she tried to slow her pulse and calm herself. She could feel Brutus watching her. She could hear him clear his throat, before making another tentative venture. "Nobody owes anyone else sexual favors," he murmured to her. "It's okay if you're not attracted to me."

She flinched, her body shuddering violently as she made a vicious little screaming noise through her teeth. "That's just it!" she snapped. "I *am* attracted to you! But... you're just too big!"

Brutus said nothing, though she knew her words must have hurt him terribly. She knew she wasn't the only one who felt self-conscious about their size. "You're big and you're handsome... I mean, you're really... but you're taller than I am, and it makes me think about... when I was..."

"Yeah. I get it." The bull's voice was gentle, filled with compassionate understanding. *And with his own pain.* She'd told him about her past trauma, about what had happened to her to leave such extensive scarring upon her psyche and her sexuality. But he didn't deserve to be compared to her abuser, and being so understanding only made him even less deserving of such treatment.

Lisa felt wretched. *This isn't fair. It isn't fair to him. It isn't fair to **me**. I shouldn't be letting **him** win again.*

Harvey had been her first consensual masculine partner, in no small part – *bad pun, that* – because he was both physically diminutive, yet also possessed of a social confidence that had allowed him to take the initiative. Gently yet daringly seducing her with an adroit awareness of her emotions, skillfully managing her personal baggage until he had her where he wanted her, with thighs spread and making eager, encouraging noises for him.

But Brutus was not Harvey, and his reluctance to make a clumsy, awkward overture was too reminiscent of... *myself.*

The thought of Brutus being made to feel as unattractive, as *unwanted*, as she so often did, proved to be the final straw. *No. Not him. He doesn't get to feel this. He's too wonderful to feel this.* It was bad enough that a long dead pirate was still reaping posthumous victories over her, casting shadows over her life. She couldn't let Brutus fall victim to the same dead monster. That vile abuser killed so long ago, by...

By the most wonderful man in the universe.

Lisa opened her eyes and turned to face Brutus. And tried not to flinch at the lonely resignation she saw in his face. "Hugging always makes me remember nice things," she declared, spreading her arms and encouraging her friend to come closer.

"Nice things, huh?" Brutus mused, as he took a step closer.

"The nicest," she agreed. There was one man who would never harm her. One man who would do anything to protect her, to make it better for her. And if there was one thing she associated with Brock, it was comforting hugs.

Brutus came within arm's reach, and then she was hugging him. Hugging him the way she hugged Brock. The way she used to hug the adults in her tribe, before... *before*. It felt good to hug him. There was nothing to associate the physical act with the abuse of her childhood. There was no triggering. Just the comforting intimacy with someone she cared for.

So what else can we do? What next? What acts had she not been forced to perform during her enslavement and torture? What could she do with Brutus, that could provide mutual pleasure and joy?

They never kissed me. Her first real kiss had been with a woman, many years later, when she was already an adult. That made sense. Kissing was too humanizing an act for the pirates to have enjoyed under any circumstances, let alone with their little "plaything." Tilting her head back to gaze up into Brutus' eyes, she curtly instructed him, "kiss me."

He did, without hesitation. There was no doubting now that he had been desiring her; his passion was undeniable. The kiss deepened, and soon their tongues were swirling... and then she realized Brutus hadn't been the one to extend a tongue and advance things further. She had. She was enjoying this. Tremendously.

Finally they came up for air, and as their heads pulled away, as they gazed into each other's eyes, Lisa felt another realization washing over her. And with it, a growing feeling of triumph.

*I'm getting turned on. I'm getting **really** turned on!*

Was it because she had become increasingly conditioned to Furries? Did his inhuman appearance circumvent her emotional triggers? Or was it simply because he was her friend, and she truly did adore him?

You know what? It doesn't matter.

Her next kiss was more aggressive, one hand reaching up to grip a horn like a handle, as she moaned into his mouth. Brutus was all but melting into her embrace, as she savored the taste of him. Until finally she pulled back, feeling a sense of elation at the awareness of her sexual arousal. Her desire for Brutus was practically a need, as if for food. It felt like a victory for her. A victory over her trauma.

Finally she pulled back, still holding his horn like a handle. "We're heading to my room," she declared, not even noticing the authoritative tone in her own voice.

Not that Brutus seemed to mind. "Yes, ma'am," he husked, looking visibly thrilled at the prospect.

Chapter 3

Lisa could only hope that nobody she knew could see her in her current state. The fact that she had been a guest at the palace for several weeks, and thus was well known to most of the staff, was irrelevant as far as her hopes were concerned. Furcadians might be as casual with sexuality as Gaians were about butchering animal carcasses, but Lisa was still decidedly the latter. Her subconscious was still wary of being teased for having obviously had sexual relations, and she was hoping to eat breakfast in peace.

The waving of hands dashed her hopes to pieces. The tall, smooth skinned figure was easily recognized from across even as large a room as what everyone insisted upon calling the cafeteria (and what Lisa insisted on calling a *royal dining hall*, at least in her own head). To make matters worse, she had caught *royal* attention. The Queen herself was waving Lisa over, and after a momentary pause to swear in the privacy of her own head, the vacationing bounty hunter limped towards Queen Bambi's table.

"This is the hero I was telling you about," the rabbit-eared, feline-fanged hybrid positively squealed to her dining companions. "The one who saved us from the BEMs, and meted out justice upon that... scurrilous pair."

"The Huntress," purred the dark furred feline woman seated between the Queen and a warmly smiling Jenny. "An honor to make your acquaintance." Lisa felt her cheeks flushing under the intent stare, as if she were a mouse cornered by a more feral – and quadrupedal – feline. "I'm Keiko," the feline added, introducing herself while staring so directly at the offworlder.

"And I'm Sally," chimed in the rabbit sitting on the other side of the Queen. Her expression seemed less predatory than that of the actual predator, but no less direct. "Why don't you join us? You look like you could stand to sit down for a bit," Sally added, with all the discretion of a hyperactive toddler on a sugar rush.

"Thanks," Lisa grumbled, sitting next to her vulpine featured friend as the usual discomfort at unexpected social interactions slithered about inside her skull. Not to mention the physical discomfort she was feeling. *Please don't let her mention it.*

Sally did not mention it. "You look like you had fun with a bull," Keiko opined, before Sally could say a word about the way the tall offworlder was moving with obvious discomfort.

Crap.

Lisa's cheeks went scarlet as she braced for the inevitable teasing. Then she paled, as Jenny squealed and reached out to grab her hand for an affectionate squeeze. "You finally did it!" Jenny enthused, her expression radiating empathetic joy. "I'm so glad for you. And for Brutus!"

Lisa struggled to keep her expression steady, as she reminded herself that this was after all Furcadia. They did things differently here. *And more often. And with more people.*

"Who is Brutus?" Sally inquired, looking politely intrigued.

"He's one of the palace custodians," the Queen interjected, providing Lisa a respite from having to answer the question. "Such a dear. Big, strong, and oh so sweet."

"Oh." Sally nodded at this description, then aimed a friendly smile in Lisa's direction. "Would you recommend him, Huntress?"

Lisa blinked and frowned in confusion at the odd question. "For what?"

Sally smiled more brightly, her expression radiating a sweet warmth as she clarified. "For what you just had!"

This is Furcadia. This is how Furries behave. Lisa had had weeks now to get accustomed to them, yet they continued to trip her up. It was one thing to be told that their culture regarded jealousy and sexual possessiveness as atavisms their society had left behind when colonizing this planet. It was another to have it casually rubbed in her face like this. *Recommend Brutus?* As if he were a piece of meat! *Well, a slab of beef.* She kept her mouth shut and nodded silently, as if to affirm that yes, Brutus was indeed worth recommending for erotic recreation.

"Hmm. Perhaps I'll look him up, while I'm here," Sally mused. Lisa suppressed the urge to snarl a possessive retort. *She's a Furry. They're Furries. Brutus would take it as a compliment.* After all, she'd been denying him her own intimacy until yesterday. Interfering with his opportunity with this rabbit would just be... *a shitty thing to do to a friend.*

Lisa was feeling herself growing increasingly introspective, losing herself in her unhappy internal musings. But weeks in this safe environment had done little to dull her paranoia, her constant, low level urge to flee or attack, and she saw the blue scaled hand before anyone else did. The waiter's reptilian lips curved in a professionally courteous smile as he set the steaming hot mug before the Queen, even as his immense round eyes aimed at Lisa like a pair of searchlights. "Would you care for your usual breakfast?" he inquired in a soft, deferential voice.

"Yes, please," Lisa agreed, grateful for the interruption from her negative internal train of thought. "Thanks, Kho."

Kho merely nodded, the nictating membranes sliding over his eyes in a lazy blink as he turned to fetch her meal. Which left Lisa on her own with two strangers as dining companions, and only one and a half friends (Lisa still had difficulty believing that a planetary leader considered her a friend, Bambi's reassurances notwithstanding) to support her through yet another social interaction.

Keiko opened the verbal interactions, sending shivers of awkward trepidation down Lisa's spine by ascribing to the common courtesy of deliberately drawing the new person into the conversation. "So, what adventures have you been having on our world, Huntress?"

Again with the lack of an honorific. They weren't addressing her as Ms Huntress, or even by her first name as they did each other. They kept addressing her as if her surname were a title. *Well, isn't it? Kind of?* "I've mostly been recovering from my last adventure," Lisa managed to stammer out. "Your world is... good for that."

"Oh, my," Keiko murmured appreciatively, leaning forward slightly with obvious interest. "What sort of heroics did you perform this time?"

A flash of appendages and spattered blood drifted past Lisa's eyes for a moment. Nor were her sensory flashbacks limited to the visual; the remembered smell of dried blood and the rancid stench of organic tissues beginning to decay and rot made her nostrils wrinkle. "I'm... not comfortable thinking about it," she mumbled, glancing down at the table.

Keiko made a soft little noise that might have been sympathy, or perhaps her own social discomfiture. Clearly she'd misstepped, though she didn't appear to understand how or why.

Jenny piped up, coming to the rescue. "So tell me again what it is you do, Keiko?" she asked politely, even as her paw slid over Lisa's hand under the table, giving it a reassuring squeeze.

"Oh," Keiko blinked, sending one more quizzical glance in Lisa's direction. "I'm the deputy administrator for Socal province," she said.

"Oh." Lisa gulped, suddenly reminded that she was, after all, sitting at the table with a planetary leader. *Of course she would be accustomed to dining with other powerful individuals.* "And... yourself?" she asked, looking over at Sally on the other side of the Queen.

Sally's sweet lapine face beamed with pride. "I'm the Sanitation Commissioner," she declared with the proud tones of someone who had earned an important position, tasked with heavy responsibilities and rewarded with lofty prestige.

"Oh," Lisa gulped. "Have I interrupted... I mean, were you were discussing business?"

Bambi interjected with a warm smile. "Remember what I told you about my royal duties?" She winked suggestively at her offworlder guest.

She did. Lisa most certainly did remember that particular conversation, when Bambi had cheerfully proclaimed herself to be a figurehead... or perhaps mediator was a better word for what she did. Managing the egos of bureaucrats, keeping them on friendly terms with each other. Preventing injured pride from causing difficulties for the rest of her society. An official charged with the overall administration of a province could have had all manner of disagreements with the person charged with the processing of waste products. Had she disturbed Bambi's deft handling of a sensitive situation, by joining them at the table?

Jenny gave her hand another gentle squeeze, then leaned in to nuzzle at her throat. Lisa shivered slightly, the embarrassment of receiving a public display of affection disrupting her train of thought. But then, Jenny worked in the palace gardens, and not as a department head. She was a gardener, one of the rank and file. Yet she was eating with the Queen?

Has Bambi been using Jenny to keep tabs on me? Lisa was uncertain how to feel about that. Was Jenny serving as a spy for the planetary leader? Not that a bounty hunter and freelance operative was a particularly valuable target, as far as Lisa could tell. Or was Bambi's interest purely affectionate? Was she truly keeping tabs on Lisa out of a sense of friendship?

Unless I'm just being paranoid. Of course, that possibility presented its own set of negative contemplations. It reaffirmed that she was beneath the notice of a Queen. Bambi had plenty of other things to concern herself with. Such as her upcoming reelection bid, which was presumably drawing near.

Lisa's mind was a whirlwind of doubts, self-recriminations, and paranoid thoughts sabotaging the very roots of her relationships. The stress of sitting with these high powered individuals was an accelerant acting upon the self-destructive process, and she didn't know how to stop it. Normally she'd attempt to politely withdraw, but that didn't seem to be an option.

Then Kho set her favorite breakfast before her, and the scent of freshly cooked animal proteins commanded her full attention. Her hands snatched up the knife and fork from her place setting, and she barely remembered to murmur a grateful noise that might have been a slurred "thank you" as she began to cut at the first of her fried eggs. Its eleven siblings glistened with a sheen of the fat they'd been fried in, the salt and spices a matte dusting atop the gloss.

Both Keiko and Sally stared, their eyes widening as they watched the Huntress greedily feasting upon a dozen eggs fried to the point of crisp crusts over their gelatinous interiors. Next to them, what appeared to be a full kilogram of sizzling hot steak awaited its turn.

"She's got large appetites," Jenny joked, grinning impishly as she lent a hint of innuendo to her words.

"No kidding," Keiko murmured, watching with awe. Sally wriggled slightly, looking almost aroused by the voracious display.

Lisa barely even noticed, as she cut away a chunk of the steak and ran it over the yolk and butter residue on the plate before popping it in her mouth. Breakfast was before her, and as preoccupied as she was with her meal she had completely forgotten her social discomfiture.

Chapter 4

It was good to have friends. Especially a friend of similar gender, someone who could serve as a guide through the world of the feminine. What little Lisa remembered of the adult women of her tribe had involved education in hunting, dressing carcasses, mathematics, science, and the history of how they had come to live in the forests of Gaia. Brock had furthered her education, teaching her the ways of technology, of maintenance and repair of ship and armor and weaponry. Tools that not only kept her alive in the harshest of environments, but also served as force multipliers for plying her trade. But Lisa had never had anyone to teach her about fashion, or flirting, or any of the nuances of courtship rituals on a Federation, planetary, or even local level.

But now she had Jenny, and Jenny was more than happy to help Lisa learn to be more alluring to those she yearned to lure. "Not that you need to," the vixen pointed out, even as she arranged yet another set of clothing upon the bed for Lisa to try on. "He's horny for you when you're wearing gym clothes and sweat." After a moment's pause, her honest nature forced her to add, "so am I."

Lisa blushed in response, but continued to follow Jenny's directives. Off came another dress, cascading down into a puddle at her feet. Apparently "loose and flowing" was insufficiently flattering. Lisa was still trying to understand what was considered flattering, but apparently she had some good qualities that needed to be emphasized. But – supposedly – that didn't mean she had bad qualities to be ashamed of, either. It simply meant that some clothing would either conceal her good qualities, create an impression that her body was less attractive than it was, or both.

Having still failed to internalize the belief that she had *any* good qualities to be emphasized, Lisa simply trusted in Jenny's judgment. Even if the next dress looked to have been sized for Jenny and not herself. It barely covered a rear that Lisa felt certain ought to be covered, and provided a similar lack of coverage for her chest. "Are you sure you got the size right?" she blurted, crossing her arms to cover the cleavage that the dress flaunted so brazenly.

"Oh, don't be like that," Jenny murmured, reaching up to gently grip Lisa's wrists and pull her arms away to her sides. She leaned in, pressing her cool wet nose against Lisa's chest, nuzzling at the smooth, furless skin. "You know how all the boys love these things," she crooned, before extending her tongue to provide a slow, languorous lick.

Lisa shivered at the sensation. "Yeah, but it's still... embarrassing..." she wavered, torn between her shyness and her trust in her friend.

"Hey, if you've got to lug these things around, you might as well get some use out of them," Jenny pointed out. Then she grinned, reaching up to press her hands into the undersides of the two hefty mounds, lifting slightly as if gauging their weight. "I mean, how heavy *are* these things? You're carrying some heavy weapons!"

That would be another thing that Lisa had never had much experience with. Casual touching. Not even sexual touching, just casual contact between friends. Touches that were friendly, comforting, or humorous. Jenny was playing with her chest as if her breasts were children's toys, and even making a goofy expression as she did so! "I wouldn't know how to weigh them," she stammered, feeling her cheeks flushing a deeper shade of red.

"You could use them to subdue a target," Jenny giggled, squeezing them together, feeling them squish through the skimpy dress. "Just slam the guy's face in between them, and demand his surrender!"

It was too easy an opportunity, and too difficult to resist the temptation. Even Lisa's formidable social awkwardness crumbled in the presence of such an obvious opening. Her hand moved almost of its own accord, as she cupped the back of Jenny's head and pulled her face in. "Surrender," she told the fox, and for a wonder her voice remained low and steady, maintaining its usual husky tones.

Jenny squealed, her arms spreading wide in momentary surprise. Then she held her hands up in a show of surrender, mumbling something that might have been sexual innuendo, and was almost certainly a declaration of submission. Lisa couldn't help but grin when she released her hold. But then, Jenny often had that effect on her.

Jenny resumed the fashion lesson, and it turned out that Lisa wouldn't have to go out in only the tight little dress after all. Arm sleeves of the same elastic material went over her limbs, sheer enough to hint at the muscular definition – particularly when she tensed her muscles at Jenny's insistence. "It's not just your tits that look amazing," she insisted.

Lisa couldn't argue with that. She was fully aware that her limbs were impressively muscled, more so than that of most men she'd met. This wasn't the first time she'd been told that it actually looked good on her, rather than being grotesquely unfeminine. But it was the first time someone had dressed her with a deliberate emphasis on them, as a putative "good quality" to be emphasized.

Leggings followed, of the same material. They covered the skin, though they hardly concealed a thing. By this point Lisa was flying blind, trusting Jenny to guide her, assuming that one of her sexual partners would know how to dress her to make her more appealing. Jenny had just begun to dip into her own personal collection of jewelry to complete the look, when Lisa's arm began to beep at her.

Jenny continued to contemplate between necklaces, chokers, and collars, as Lisa pulled back the arm sleeve to expose her forearm. The pseudoflesh of her prosthetic limb barely hinted at a seam, until she lifted up what looked like a flap of skin over rigid plastic, revealing her commlink. In a technologically advanced society, there were the occasional advantages to being an amputee. She peered down at the screen, reading the message. And the identity of the sender.

"Damn it," she muttered quietly.

Jenny looked up in surprise.

"I've just been handed an assignment by the FIA," Lisa explained, lowering the cover and slipping the sleeve back into place.

"I thought you were a private contractor?" Jenny said.

"Yeah, but I'm on permanent retainer now," Lisa sighed. Ever since her last encounter with the Fey had made it painfully evident that her harassment would be a continuing thing, the available options had been explored. The optimal choice, one that respected her personal freedoms as well as the strategic opportunities presented, was to make her a stalking goat. Though to be fair, being on retainer with the FIA did offer numerous benefits.

Aren't I lucky? So nice to have a hive minded collective consciousness for a stalker. Lisa had had more interaction with the ancient enemies of humanity than any single individual had in a thousand years. The Overone, the name claimed by the collective intelligence of that unspeakable species, had deemed her a threat for her ability to resist the paralytic effects of its telepathic assault. She had no way of knowing what it might attempt next, in its ongoing efforts to break her, kill her, or otherwise render her incapable of spreading that ability to others.

"So when do you have to leave?" Jenny asked, visibly crestfallen.

"Tomorrow," Lisa grumbled, before attempting to rally. "But we can still enjoy tonight."

"Hmm," Jenny mused, her furry forehead furrowing with the effort of thought. "Maybe we could have a foursome to say goodbye? I could see if Harvey's free tonight."

The very notion was akin to being suddenly seized and hurled into a warm, sweetly scented bubble bath. As lovely as the prospect might have been, it was still very much outside Lisa's comfort zone, particularly when she hadn't been expecting it. A romantic evening with Brutus had been very much part of Lisa's plans. A romantic evening with Harvey would have been a delightful surprise. A romantic evening with Jenny was always a welcome experience. But all four of them together was something Lisa felt ought to be carefully worked into, after sufficient time to get used to it.

Perhaps her distress was evident in her expression. Jenny reached up to gently caress Lisa's cheek as she hastily amended, "How about you just let your friends perform for you? You can watch the show, until you feel like joining in." It was a sweet suggestion, one that sounded sincere and considerate, showing a sensitivity to her offworlder inhibitions.

It also sounded like something for her nagging self-doubts to seize upon. "Are... are you thinking to take a turn with Brutus?" Lisa couldn't help but ask, as pangs of jealousy shot through her. Immediate remorse compelled her to hastily add, in an attempt to sound less accusatory, "while I watch?"

Jenny just giggled and winked suggestively. Perhaps it had flown right over her head. Sexual possessiveness was almost unheard of on this planet, it was possible that a cultural misunderstanding had saved her friend from hurt feelings. Lisa added another suggestion to further smooth it over, "or did you want to have fun with Harvey?"

Jenny grinned, her white fangs gleaming in her muzzle as her other hand began to slide over Lisa's hip. "Actually, I was thinking I'd cuddle up with you, while we watch Harvey and Brutus put on the show."

The room began to tilt slightly, as if the artificial gravity were on the fritz. *No, wait. I'm on a planet.* Lisa realized she was swaying, reeling from the suggestion. Harvey, slender, short, vigorous Harvey. Brutus, tall and muscular and magnificent. She attempted to form a response, but all that came out was a babbled bit of gibberish. "What... uh.. who... I mean... which one... uh..."

Jenny giggled as she pressed in closer. "You mean, who's going to penetrate who?" she asked teasingly.

Lisa gulped and nodded mutely, even as her brain, addled as it was by the unexpected suggestions, tried to calculate the necessary geometric equations. Her imagination failed to process how Brutus might be "topped" by a male half his height. Whereas the reverse – Harvey allowing Brutus to penetrate him with that bovine phallus – didn't seem possible according to the known laws of physics.

Jenny leaned in to nuzzle at Lisa's chest, planting a soft kiss upon the breasts she'd been having so much fun with. "Knowing them, they'll take turns," she reflected. "It's always fun to watch."

Lisa stared up at the ceiling, her legs having suddenly given way beneath her. The bed's exquisite mattress absorbed the impact with ease; it took her a moment to realize what had just happened.

Jenny giggled and pulled away, enjoying her large friend's shocked, overwhelmed expression and demeanor. "Now come on, let's pick out a nice necklace," she snickered. "We're going to give you a proper sendoff."

Chapter 5

Consoles and control schemes were both standardized and diverse, after a millennia of experience with what worked and what didn't. Test pilots had died because what engineers thought looked good in a design schematic turned out to have unforeseen drawbacks. Modern cockpit designs relied primarily on touchscreen interfaces; at a whim the displayed surface could become a keyboard, a succession of windowed folders, a pointer icon to be slid about with a single fingertip. Lisa could control her vessel as if it were an old atmospheric fighter craft, allow the computer to handle the piloting while she busied herself with weaponry or other equipment, or simply set the *Hearth* to accelerate and coast towards a safe distance from gravity wells before jumping to a new system.

The latter of course left her free to slip over to the galley and make herself some hot cocoa. The ship's kitchen was of course fully furnished; even the cheapest of vessels included a fully automated suite of culinary devices. Compared to the cost of the hyperspace engines that laughed in the face of physics and told the fabric of space-time to get bent, a rectangular box that drew water from the ship's stores, heated it to boiling, then mixed it with powders before dispensing a filled squeezebulb was a pittance to supply. Lisa gave her bulb a very gentle squeeze, sipping the scalding hot liquid with practiced ease.

Too bad you can't get whipped cream in a squeezebulb. The standard beverage container aboard both vessels and space habitats, made of flexible and temperature resistant polymers, and shaped something like a flat bottomed globe with a nipple at the top, was a holdover from the days when people were nervous about artificial gravity failures. They continued to be used as tradition, and were optimal for safely carrying drinks without risk of untidy spills. But sadly, there was no way to furnish the accompaniments that an open topped cup could offer. Lisa sipped her whipped cream-less, marshmallow-bereft cocoa as she touched the primary galley console.

I feel like having some fried roots.

That would take a little while longer; while prepared and preserved meals were always available, Lisa had always favored freshly cooked food. The kitchen devices were of course up to the task, but it would still take time. And so while the carrots, potatoes, and yams were extracted from within the galley's stores and sliced into batonnet strips, Lisa sat down at the small but serviceable kitchen table with her cocoa and a tablet, to begin reviewing the details of her assignment.

My first FIA assignment on permanent retainer. She was definitely advancing, professionally. Her first contract for the Federation Intelligence Agency had been meant as a test of her abilities, probing what had been assumed to be simple corruption. The discovery of a Fey conspiracy had come as a considerable surprise to everyone involved (including the Fey, who had been most upset about being discovered). This would be her first job as an officially approved contractor, specifically called out to handle a task requiring someone with her abilities and skillset.

A few meters away, the batonnet cut root vegetables were being moved through the suite of interconnected devices underneath the galley counter, relocated from the slicer to the pressure cooker. Water was being heated to the boiling point, spraying into the cut vegetables within that pressurized container. As the vegetables were steamed, Lisa dragged her finger along the tablet's surface, reading through the materials provided.

The squeezebulb demonstrated its practicality as it fell to the floor; only a tiny spurt of hot dark liquid spat out when it landed. It rolled a half a meter before Lisa snatched it up, her initial startlement immediately giving way to her more usual sense of panic and social paranoia. She took the time to wipe up the minor mess, allowing her to attempt to come to terms with her sentiments regarding the matter.

This has got to be a joke.

The worst part was knowing that she couldn't decline the assignment, particularly not when she'd already acknowledged the commission and provided an ETA for her arrival. She should have read the details first. She really ought to have read the details first. *Didn't they read **my** file? I hunt fugitives!*

But it was *fait accompli*. Someone had apparently decided that Lisa Huntress, paranoid introvert and social recluse, was just the sort of person they wanted to conduct a murder investigation. Someone had actually drawn the conclusion that someone with serious psychological issues and the lifestyle of a nocturnal solitary predator was the right choice to wander around a densely populated colony, having intense conversations with large numbers of random strangers and asking tactful questions about sensitive subjects.

Lisa stood there with her cocoa in hand, staring at nothing as she tried to will the situation to be different. Though she had no way of knowing, her vegetables had finished steaming and were being blasted with heated air to dry them, by the time she sat back down again and resumed reading in the hopes that the text had changed since she'd first scanned it.

It hadn't. *Crap.*

She continued to read, hoping to find a silver lining in this dark cloud. *Perhaps it's a sparsely populated colony. Maybe it's just a research facility, even!*

It was not a research facility. There were several hundred thousand colonists already present; the colony was on its third generation. A fairly new world, as far as the Federation was concerned, yet already large enough for the initial colony to have begun to branch out, forming the capital of a larger civilization. As the hot oil jetted into the pressure cooker and hit the steam-softened vegetables, Lisa reeled under the impact of knowing she would have to undergo the extreme stress of prolonged social interactions with the residents of the planet Wigglebiggle.

Wigglebiggle.

Lisa stared at the far wall for a moment. Then she looked back down at the tablet, reading the name for a third time. *Wigglebiggle. They actually named their world... Wigglebiggle.*

*Now I **know** this has to be a joke.*

It was not a joke. The planet had initially been named Varuna, until the discovery of a... *crap.* Despite her own distress, Lisa felt stirred into sympathy towards the beleaguered colonists. *Someone screwed up. Someone screwed up **big.***

The Federation had grown as large, as powerful, and as prosperous as it had, in no small part due to its reliance on ancient history as a moral compass. Past civilizations provided a rich plethora of examples of what not to do, and while there might be plenty of room for individual worlds to have their own unique societies, some things were universally understood as a bad idea. Chief among those being: colonialism. The inevitable harm that accrued to both parties, whenever a technologically advanced society invaded and subjugated a less advanced culture. For starters, how the oppression of the indigenous people reinforced the hierarchy of the oppressive society. A soldier of the British Empire might have felt superior to the natives during his posting abroad, but he would have internalized his own role as a victim of the wealthy aristocrats who pilfered and appropriated from his fellow Londoners as readily as they did the Indians he'd been taught to look down upon.

No, there were a host of reasons why Federation citizens were forbidden from establishing colonies upon worlds known to have a sapient native species. Even if that native species were still in the rock throwing stage of development. Even if that native species were completely inhuman in nature. It was still their world, and the Federation had been founded in a deliberate rejection of archaic bigotry. *We have nicer toys than you do. You're different from us. That gives us the right to take whatever you have that we want.* The mentality of a colonizer. The mentality of a corporate raider. Of a narcissistic autocrat. A criminal.

The mentality of a pirate.

The entire planet should have been evacuated. That would have been the usual response, particularly for newly formed colonies. But it had taken three generations before the colonists had realized that the oceans of their new world harbored sapient life. In shockingly large numbers, at that. The Octopussies were estimated to number in the tens of millions...

*This has **got** to be a joke!* Lisa felt like screaming. Someone had to be pulling her leg. *This is ridiculous! It's an elaborate hoax... the Fey. It has to be the Fey.*

That actually cheered her a bit. If it really was a hoax, she could simply go in with weapons hot, kill everything in front of her, and call it a day. She could hope. Oh, how she could hope.

The galley chimed at her, informing her that her food was finally ready. The fried root vegetables were ready to be plated and eaten, having been fried, air-blasted clear of the majority of the dripping oil, and seasoned. She rose up to fetch her snack, bringing it back to the table in a bowl, with a squeezebulb filled with ketchup.

The fried food made her feel better, as rich fatty carbs generally did. She nibbled at a piece of deep fried potato, encrusted with salt and topped with ketchup as she skipped ahead to the information regarding the... Octopussies. *Anatomically similar to the Terran octopus. Hmm.* She opened a second window on the tablet, checking for encyclopedia information on the octopus. *Long tentacles.* Ick. *Exceptional intelligence. Creates ink to spray for defensive purposes. Venomous bite... ink **and** venom?* The Terran octopus had been endowed with quite the arsenal by evolution. Did the Octopussies of Wigglebiggle possess similar abilities?

For that matter, would she ever get used to using the words "Octopussies" and "Wigglebiggle" in the same sentence, without feeling like an idiot?

Going back to her mission files proved fruitless, in regards to answering either question. Whatever abilities the Octopussies might have were still being ascertained. What was confirmed was that – unlike the Terran octopus – they not only survived the reproductive act, they were naturally extremely long lived. Plenty of lifespan for learning new things. Plenty of opportunity to pass on knowledge to future generations. More than sufficient for the creation of a culture, of a society.

Lisa felt sickly certain as to why the information regarding this species was so critical. She skipped back to the details regarding the murder itself, and her suspicions were confirmed. *Crap!*

Of course the victim was an Octopussy. *Not just **an** Octopussy. **The** Octopussy.* The ambassador to the colony, as the two societies had attempted to come to an understanding, a possible solution that involved the human colonists remaining as welcome neighbors.

This has to be a sick prank. The Overone's trying to drive me to suicide. She was going to make extensive use of her gravitic lance! She was going to slaughter everyone involved in this charade! She was going to do... *nothing of the sort. This is real. I have to accept it.*

Crap.

She bit down on two sticks at once, tasting both carrot and sweet potato as she chewed. The mild sweetness cut through the ketchup as she self-medicated with the delicious greasy snack. Then she took a sip of hot cocoa to wash it down, before setting the squeezebulb down next to the container of ketchup. Chocolate and fatty carbs, a two-hit combination assault against her emotional distress.

I can do this. I have to do this. Her career was on the rise, but that meant overcoming new challenges. She couldn't simply coast on her previous accomplishments and never achieve anything new. If that meant leaving her comfort zone, then she'd simply have to get used to being uncomfortable.

After all... She sighed and closed her eyes, forehead furrowed with frustration. *They need me. Or someone a lot better than me, but I'm what they'll have to settle for.* She kept her eyes shut, as if the light hurt them, while reaching out to take another sip of her cocoa.

Lisa was already speculating, contemplating methods of dealing with the situation. First and foremost, she would need a way to bypass her usual social ineptitude. Her previous attempts at investigation and interrogation had proven disastrously inept — the memory of her humiliating interactions with a detainee on New Athens was always waiting to remind her of how badly she'd screwed up — and she needed a means of managing her personal issues so she could do the job.

She had always needed some sort of protective barrier between herself and the multitudes of society. Physical distance, tangible barriers, an armor against the social interactions that she was still so fearful of.

Then the solution came to her, like a sudden beam of light from above. It was... *perfect. I can make it into a signature of sorts. Part of my style.* Yes, that would work. Eccentricity was always tolerated in the competent. As long as she could be competent, she could get away with a little eccentricity.

Feeling quite pleased with herself for coming up with such a clever solution, Lisa tilted her head back and squeezed hard for a prolonged sip of the contents of her squeezebulb.

Fortunately the squeezebulb concept really was a very practical design. It didn't take her too long to clean up the mouthful of ketchup she had spat out across the room.

Chapter 6

Patrick loved his truck.

If you had asked him his reasons for being so fond of his vehicle, he wouldn't have been able to talk about its magnetic suspension, a centuries old design that relied on "room temperature" superconductors to provide a stable, reliable means of providing a smooth ride. He couldn't have spoken about the make and model of the motors that made its wheels roll, because he didn't know them. Particularly since they'd been replaced with upgraded versions a half dozen times over its lifetime. He couldn't even recall offhand how many kilometers it could travel on a single charge.

What he could have said was that it was as old as the colony. His grandfather had relied on it for decades, before his mother had inherited it. To Patrick it was an heirloom, as if his grandfather was still taking care of him years after the old man had passed on. Right now it was taking care of both Patrick and Chun, ensuring they could keep their appointment.

"This is it," Chun announced, as Patrick brought the truck to a stop in front of the freshly descended vessel.

"Not a bad little ship," Patrick conceded, opening the driver's side door and sliding out. He glanced up with mild interest, taking in the curvature of the solid looking spacecraft. Work roughened hands pressed themselves to the fabric of his pants as he did his best to assume a suitably commanding stance befitting Wigglebiggle's governor.

Even if I'm still thinking of myself as the governor of Varuna.

"It's an Elite 2500 XT," his Chief Jingcha went on, her own eyes staring with a considerably more avid interest. "They were churning out thousands of these, about eighty years ago."

"Between the 2400 and the 2600, right?" Patrick quipped.

Chun appeared to have missed his attempt at a joke. "The design is centuries old," she continued to comment on their guest's craft. "They try to make improvements every now and then, but it's still the same basic design. For small crews living on the ship for weeks at a time."

Patrick nodded, his gaze focused on what was presumably the hatch their guest would be emerging from. "You've been doing your homework on them," he intuited.

"I've been doing my homework on our new investigator," Chun retorted. "She's called... the Huntress."

Patrick glanced at Chun, one bushy brow arched in inquiry. "By who?" he murmured, sounding slightly amused at such a dramatic appellation.

"Everyone," Chun breathed.

Patrick's other eyebrow rose to join the first, in response to her awed, breathless tone.

"She's an expert on investigations," Chief Jingcha Chun Callan went on, staring at the hatch with what Patrick considered to be a rather unusual level of nervous awe. Her stocky, well muscled body was positively vibrating with barely contained excitement. "She uncovered a massive Fey conspiracy back on Earth."

"On Earth? Old Earth?" Patrick blinked with shock at the revelation. "The Fey managed to start something on... Earth?" he asked, in much the same way that a man living in Poland in the twenty-first century might have reacted to news that the Mongols had just invaded Warsaw.

"Didn't you hear? It was all over the news," Chun chided him.

"So's a lot of other stuff," Patrick retorted defensively.

"It was a big scandal at the time," Chun went on, and despite her age she sounded like a teenaged girl obsessing over her favorite musician. "Then she uncovered *another* Fey conspiracy on New Athens, just a few months later. If *she's* the one doing the hunting, the culprit's as good as caught."

Patrick nodded solemnly, acknowledging this declaration of his top security official's opinion regarding the FIA operative. "Sounds like someone's got a *cruuuuush*..." he sang out.

Chun's cheeks flushed a dark brownish red. "Goon," she grumbled. Then the ship's hatch opened, and the both of them ceased their friendly bickering and braced to greet their guest.

Holy...!

Patrick had to admit that, when he'd sent out the request for assistance, he'd expected something decidedly... different. Not quite as tall, for one thing. Something more sociable in appearance. Something wearing a form of cloth. The armored figure stepping down the ramp looked less like a brilliant sleuth and more like a bipedal combat drone built by someone with a large budget and a murderous grudge. Despite its sheer size, the figure moved with an uncommon grace; each step landed with only a slight thud, rather than the resounding boom he would have expected.

Yet for some reason, Chun didn't appear to be remotely surprised. Awed, certainly. But hardly surprised. Not even by the way one arm terminated in a curious cylindrical shape, devoid of either gauntlet, or a hand to stick in said gauntlet. She merely watched with wide eyes as the figure stalked towards them, the heavy looking duffel bag clutched by the other hand slowly swaying with each step. Finally the soft thuds ended several meters from the greeting party, and silence fell.

The silence extended on, as Patrick stared up at the mirrored surface of the figure's helmet. It seemed that this *Huntress* was the silent type. *Or perhaps she's just trying to posture?* It wouldn't be out of place for someone calling themselves by such a flashy title. But he was the governor, and it fell to him to show proper hospitality. "Welcome to Wigglebiggle. I'm Governor Patrick Chu," he declared, offering a slight bow at the waist.

The armored behemoth regarded him in silence for a moment, before mimicking his bow. "Hello."

Her voice was... big. Not necessarily loud, but certainly sounding capable of becoming loud. The sort of voice one associated with large chests and powerful diaphragms. Of course that could have been due to a voice synthesizer, yet there was a sense of fullness to the voice that left Patrick fairly certain that she would have sounded much the same, even without the armor. If anything, it reminded him of his mother's voice. "This is Chun Callan, Chief Jingcha," he went on, waving a hand in the direction of the stocky, middle aged woman. "The Jingcha are our local law enforcement."

Chun bowed rather more deeply than Patrick had, murmuring her greeting, "Welcome to Wigglebiggle." If she was embarrassed about having to call their homeworld by that name, it did not show.

The colossus returned Chun's bow, before straightening up to regard them both in silence. Chun smiled, and Patrick couldn't help but notice the shy hopefulness in that expression. *Bloody cao, I think she really **does** have a crush!* But the Huntress wasn't saying anything, and the silence was uncomfortable, oppressive.

Which fell to Patrick to resolve, as the host of hosts. It was up to him to act in a hospitable fashion. "If you'll hop in," he suggested, waving at his beloved truck, "we'll take you to the lodgings we've prepared for you, for as long as you'll be staying with us."

"Thank you." The FIA operative stalked towards the truck, and suddenly Patrick recognized an issue. Simply put, the vehicle didn't have enough room in the main cab for all three of them. It barely had enough room for the armored figure by herself, and only if they first removed the seats. He opened his mouth, trying to think of a solution to suggest, but the Huntress had already found one.

Huh. Maybe she's not such a diva after all. It certainly was a practical solution, and one that he wouldn't have dared to suggest lest he offend. He returned to the driver side and hopped in, while the Huntress shifted her armored bulk to find a comfortable position in the truck's bed.

Chun gripped the handle of the opposite door, then hesitated. "Would you like me to keep you company back there?" she offered.

The Huntress leaned against the back of the cab, now comfortably sprawled out and with her duffel bag nestled between her thick, heavily armored thighs. "You'll be more comfortable in the cab," she suggested. "Thank you, though."

Patrick bit his lip and tried not to react to the look of disappointment on Chun's face. They'd been friends for a long time, and he could get away with teasing her when few others could – but there were limits, and she still knew how to knock someone on their ass with one blow. Instead he turned on the power and started the drive to the barracks, while behind him the fabled *Huntress* sat, no doubt taking in the sights of their beautiful world.

He hoped they'd still be able to call it their world, a year from now.

Chapter 7

As governor, Patrick had felt obliged to serve as a tour guide of sorts, maintaining a constant patter during the drive from the spaceport to the municipal buildings. Of course it had been a trip of less than a kilometer, but it was still long enough for him to point out the better eating establishments and what they offered, and the silk factory that promised to become the start of a booming export business. There were a few clothing shops with window displays of silk and wool, ideal for wet, often chilly conditions. And of course, there were the municipal buildings, where Patrick spent, in his own words, far too much time. They formed a series of rounded bubbles, geodesic domes constructed at the founding of the colony. The truck pulled up to a halt before one such dome, and Patrick shut off the engine as he announced, "we're here. The Gonganting. The Jingcha barracks," he clarified. "It's where most of the unmarried Jingcha live."

"Most?" the armored figure asked, as it slowly maneuvered its way out of the back of the truck. She appeared to be taking care to avoid damaging the vehicle; Patrick felt grateful for that.

"There's always someone wanting more privacy," Chun explained, stepping around the vehicle to wait by the back. She watched as the armored operative carefully climbed out, keeping her expression as formally polite as possible.

"I see," Lisa grunted, retrieving her bag before turning to face not only Chun, but also the building behind her.

"We assumed you'd want lodgings close to the governor's office and the other critical facilities, while you're handling your investigation," Chun added hastily. "I've taken the liberty of assigning you the room next to mine. That... that's okay, right?"

"That's fine," Lisa replied, adjusting the strap of her duffel bag to slide it over her forearm. "Please, just show me the way," she requested, carrying the heavy bag as if it were an evening purse.

Patrick couldn't help but grin as he watched Chun leading the way to the front door, then down the halls to the rooms in question. "Here's your passkey," the Chief Jingcha said, offering Lisa a slip of plastic. "You can copy it at your leisure."

The Huntress carefully took it between her thumb and index finger, taking visible pains to avoid harming the other woman with her augmented strength. "Thank you." She waved the plastic in the general direction of the door, and as the lock chimed that it had been released she slid it open. One massive boot stepped into the room, before the figure halted. "So what time should we meet up?"

Behind Chun, Patrick's jaw dropped. Chun herself stammered in shock, "meet up...?"

"To begin the investigation," the Huntress clarified.

"Oh." Chun was trying not to sound crestfallen, coughing

to clear her throat. "Ahem. Yes, I've had my schedule cleared. We can meet up whenever you're ready."

"I will." The Huntress began to slide the door closed, then stopped. "Actually... there is one other thing."

Chun arched a brow and kept her face as impassive as possible. "Yes?"

The helmet tilted as the armored figure looked down at her. "Is there..." She trailed off, leaving the question unfinished.

After a few seconds Chun gently prodded, "yes?"

The Huntress continued to loom silently for a time, before finally asking the question. "Is there... a place, where I can order takeout food?"

Chapter 8

Now that she was alone, Lisa finally felt safe exiting her armor. The gleaming old workhouse of a suit opened with a soft hiss, as she slipped out like a molting insect shedding the carapace it had outgrown. The duffel bag she'd hauled from the *Hearth* contained both her prosthetic hand and the power cord for her suit; after attaching the former to her stump she attached the latter to both suit and power outlet.

Next came the simple task of copying her passkey. The plastic slip had had a lovely looking example of what appeared at first to be a sort of fractal geometry etched onto its surface. A matrix code, to be scanned by her door's sensor. A thousand years since the invention of optical scanners had yielded tremendous improvements to the fundamental design. Merely waving the card in the general direction of the door was sufficient.

But scanning the matrix code onto her own personal area network meant that she didn't even need to do that much. Once she'd copied the code, she could unlock her door simply by approaching it with her suit or her prosthetic limb. The card itself could be left on the desk; no doubt it would be melted down and the lock reset after her departure.

Now that that was taken care of, she finally felt free to de-stress. First by flopping onto the bed, giving it a proper stress test. Then by breathing deeply, deliberately working to steady her heart. *Deep breaths. Deep breaths.* It had been one of the first lessons she'd learned during her years of therapy. Growing up with Brock, her foster father and mentor, had meant a lack of permanent residence, but he'd selected a qualified therapist capable of treating her via remote sessions. *Control your breathing. Control your heart rate. Control your physiology.*

It hadn't exactly been difficult to diagnose her issues, or even to analyze their root cause. Her earliest years had been spent within the loving confines of a small social grouping. For a small child growing up in the hunter-gatherer culture of Gaia, the world was the bright warmth of the sacred hearth's fire, and everything away from that fire was darkness and danger, the dim light poking through the canopy of the giant trees providing scarcely sufficient illumination for a human ill-adapted by genetic drift. Even with her eyes naturally adapted to the local conditions, Gaia's forests were a place where one wrong step could lead to falling from a branch hundreds of meters above the inky blackness of the forest floor, or triggering an ambush predator such as a monkey spider. Children were kept close, the entire community numbering perhaps a dozen or so adults, perhaps twice that number of children. For a little girl, the entire universe was populated by a dozen loving parents and her siblings. Everything else was the scary unknown.

And then the scary unknown had taken all of that away. The first people Lisa had ever met outside of her tribe, aside from the occasional Elder visiting from another tribe or

Wandering in search of a new tribe to settle with, had been the pirates who had taken... *everything.*

She had spent a year with them, learning what true evil was, before Brock had avenged her tribe and saved most of her. By which time she had fully internalized the subconscious certainty that everything outside the protection of a parental figure was scary, cruel, and evil. Small wonder she only felt comfortable in her armor, or at the very least aboard her ship. It had been the *Helldorado* before it had been rechristened the *Hearth*, and both armor and vessel were tangible links to her sole remaining parent.

And so she breathed, hearkening to the lessons from her earliest therapy sessions. Doctor Singh had provided Lisa with basic tools for coping with her chronic issues. *Your brain is an organic computer, powered and sustained by the chemicals your body feeds it. Control your physiology, and control your mind. Deep breaths. Steady pulse. You're not in danger. No flight. No fight. Calm. Clear thinking.*

Lisa continued to breathe, fighting her own body's yearning to remain solidly in fight-or-flight mode in response to the intense stress of social interaction. Another deep inhalation. Holding her breath for a brief period. Exhaling, slowly and steadily. Another inhalation. Hold. Release. Again. And again. Like any other person suffering from a chronic condition, Lisa had learned and practiced her regimen until it was as automatic as reaching for her prosthetic limb, or cleaning her teeth.

I can do this.

The governor was a rough featured fellow, but Lisa was more than comfortable around such types. He reminded her enough of Brock that it was almost comforting. But his law enforcement head had left Lisa feeling glad that she'd decided to adopt an "eccentric" persona and make her armor a part of her mystique.

She'd spent the entire ride with the sense of having the attention of a predator, her tribal instincts sending alarms from the back of her mind. To say nothing of the woman's aggressive interest. Lisa felt as if she were being treated as a suspect for whatever unsolved cases remained in the Jingcha's files.

The sound of several chimes ringing in succession, came from the door, one of the typical default ringtones for doors and commlinks since time immemorial. Before the second note had struck Lisa was already facing the door in a half crouch, responding with the reflexes that no sane person would ever want to possess, if they knew the price. "Who..." she yelped, then took a deep breath and tried again, forcing herself to speak more calmly and in a normal tone of voice. "Who is it?"

"Jingcha Stevens, Huntress," a young man's voice called out. "I've brought the meals you requested."

Well. There it was, the reason why her conditioned reflexes often proved such a liability. She took another deep breath, then another, before she dared to approach the door. One hand slid it partially open, keeping it as a barrier between herself and the jingcha, even as she peered around the corner to catch a glimpse of him. His own expression remained professionally stoic even as his eyes widened slightly. He tilted his head back to look up at the eyes and forehead peering down at him from above, even as he held out the plastic bag gripped in his fist.

"Thanks," she muttered as she snatched the bag away; his fingers opened just in time to avoid having any of them dislocated from the sudden yank. Then followed a brief period of awkwardness, Lisa feeling certain that more was expected of her, yet uncertain as to what. "Um... thank you," she repeated, before sliding the door shut.

Well, that went about as well as it usually does. Once again she'd had a casual social interaction with a random stranger that left her feeling humiliated and ashamed, as if she'd screwed up something of critical importance. But no sense crying over spilled milk, not when she had better things to spill. Or at least, to dispense. The bag was set upon the desk and three rectangular boxes were extracted, each of them smelling excitingly of delicious food.

Opening the first left her presented with a note from whatever dining establishment had been tasked with providing the takeout order that the intimidating law enforcement chief had promised to have brought to her. *Due to recent events, fish will no longer be served*, the note read. *We apologize for the inconvenience. Instead of our world famous Surf Special, please enjoy our Meat Lover's Banquet.*

Well. That sounded pretty good. The bottom of the box itself was completely covered in a thick layer of rice, topped with a selection of thinly sliced meats of various animals. Land dwelling creatures, clearly. Lisa split the provided chopsticks and snatched up a slice of something glistening with sauce, taking a greedy bite.

Bison. Yum! She hadn't had bison since her last visit to Lonestar. She took another bite, chewing with gusto as she began to consume her first Meat Lover's Banquet. Bison, beef, pork, and mutton all played together on her taste buds as they were chewed thoroughly and swallowed so hungrily. The rice was filling and delicious, the sauce soaking into the grains to lend a rich flavor to the tasty side dish. It didn't take long before she was reduced to chasing the last few grains around the bottom of the container, feeling more or less replete. At least, for now. She could save the second container for later, as a late snack before sleeping. The third would suffice for an early breakfast, before she donned her armor to begin the day.

In the meantime, she ought to do some preliminary work. Retrieving her tablet from the duffel bag, she laid back on the bed, her back propped up by a few pillows and the wall. *I should start by learning more about the layout of the capital.*

After all, it was useful to know the layout of the terrain, when hunting.

Chapter 9

Even in a small, youngish colony such as Varuna – er, Wigglebiggle – there were benefits to having a position of authority. Even if it was something so simple as the first pick of the morning biscuits to go with a hot cup of tea. Even if the price of getting to snatch at the selection before anyone else was starting the day before anyone else. A couple pieces of shortbread could keep a Chief going until she had the opportunity for a proper meal.

Chun was decidedly impressed, when the bounty hunter pushed her office door open and stalked into the room. At least two hundred kilos of armored amazon had just entered, and yet her footsteps were almost silent. By all rights the woman should have been announcing her approach with a succession of percussive thuds, yet she moved with a predatory grace even in that armor.

The Huntress stopped a few meters from her desk, standing there as if at attention. "Chief Jingcha Callan," she said, her courteous tones amplified by her armor's audio output.

"Call me Chun," the Chief replied, trying to make her

smile seem warm and friendly, rather than shy or nervous. "Would you care for some tea? A biscuit?"

"I've eaten," Lisa replied shortly, holding her posture stiff and unmoving. "Thank you."

"All right," Chun replied agreeably, popping the rest of the biscuit she'd been nibbling on into her mouth. She chewed it thoroughly as she stared up at the helmet's visage, waiting for the Huntress to say something. Then she swallowed, regarding the tall, armored woman standing there as they continued to stare at each other in silence. When the silence began to feel too awkward to remain silent, Chun gulped, "Er... so where did you want to start?"

The Huntress answered the question without hesitation. "I want to start by learning everything you can tell me, about the victim."

Well. Chun felt both intimidated and reassured. The FIA had definitely sent someone who knew what they were doing. The Huntress seemed to radiate a cool professionalism that Chun couldn't help but envy. "If I'm going to do that..." she began, then trailed off in sudden thought. "I'm going to have to explain about the Octopussies, first."

The Huntress promptly responded, "please tell me about the Octopussies, then."

Chun opened her mouth. Then she shut it, frowning thoughtfully. "I think..." she considered it. There really wasn't a way to do them justice, with words alone. Yes, the Huntress would just have to get to know them personally. *Besides, I want to see how she handles it.* "It's probably best to introduce you to one," Chun finally suggested.

"Are Octopussies and humans still interacting, after what happened?" The Huntress sounded surprised. Not without reason, given that an ambassador had been murdered.

"Oh, yes," Chun replied. "To be honest... well, I'll explain after you've met him. We have an Octopussy serving as a deputy Jingcha." *Sort of.*

The armored figure loomed for several long moments, clearly digesting this information and extrapolating possibilities. "All right. Please introduce me to him."

It wasn't a long walk, by any means. The initial colony, the capital, had been built near to the shore for optimal access to a diverse array of resources. Between the municipal buildings and the ocean were the docks (where all the aquatic vessels, public as well as private, had been restricted until they could determine property rights and easements), and between the docks and the municipal buildings there was a massive tank filled with seawater. In the absence of silt or other deposits, there was nothing to leave the water clouded. The liquid was as clear as bathwater, revealing the swirling mess of tentacles idly pirouetting about.

The Huntress froze in midstride, staring at the aquatic alien in rapt silence. Chun continued to approach, nonchalantly waving her hand in a warm greeting to her "special" deputy.

Which provided a perfect handle for a tentacle to latch onto.

Behind her, the Huntress gave a grunt of shock and surprise as Chun was lifted off her feet, hauled bodily towards the tank by the suckered tentacle wrapped around her wrist. As Chun was pulled towards the rim of the tank, a deep, booming voice declared, in the sepulchral tones of an inquisitor passing out judgment, "**you're *nicked*, chum**!"

Chapter 10

Behind her, Chun could hear the unmistakable sound of a very idiosyncratic weapon being activated. A weapon that was almost never used as one. "Lightsabers," as they were known, created charged particle fields of atomic scale cross section, fields that rotated at relativistic speeds to create "blades" that tore apart molecules. They were primarily used in mining and construction, but there were always a few eccentrics who found them fascinating enough to carry around as weaponry. *And the Huntress has one in that **gunhand** of hers.* "Don't! It's okay!" she cried out hastily, waving frantically with her free hand at the charging figure.

The Huntress ceased her abrupt forward movement, though whether she was ceasing her attack or waiting for an opportunity was unclear. Chun would have to act quickly. "Jingcha Tako!" she shouted, in her best *I am your boss* voice, "Let go of your Chief!"

The tentacle unwound from her wrist, slipping back beneath the surface of the seawater. Chun came to a halt with her hands outstretched to break her forward momentum against the transparent wall of the tank. She took a moment to catch her breath, then glared over her shoulder at the Huntress. "It's okay," she repeated, in case the Huntress were inclined to believe otherwise.

Tako's voice boomed out again, the grumpy grumbling of an annoyed pagan deity. "**You're still under arrest.**"

"Yeah?" Chun breathed, glaring into the depths of the tank. She could see one of his large eyes, and glared directly at it. "What are you trying to arrest me for?"

The tentacles swirled slowly in the water, as Tako declared in a loud, crisply articulated voice, "**You are in violation of statute Forty Three, of the Wigglebiggle Animal and Livestock code.**"

"Yeah?" Chun prodded, still glaring into his eye.

"**According to statute Forty Three, I am required to have a selection of toys, or other forms of entertainment, for my holding pen.**" Tako's words slammed down like the gavel of a judge wanting to throw the book at the convicted felon standing before him.

"Yeah?" Chun repeated, before retorting, "that code applies to livestock and pets. Which you are neither. You're a sapient being, punk! And you're a Jingcha on duty! You're subject to Gongating regulations!" She made a point of rubbing her wrist where he'd grabbed her, snapping out each word crisply. "And that means you don't! Grab! Your! Chief!"

Two of the tentacles passed in front of his eye, as he broke from her direct glare. "**Well, I still want a toy!**" he sulked.

Chun sighed, then glanced over her shoulder at the Huntress. Who was still frozen in position, lightsaber still blazing furiously as it stripped apart the molecules coming into contact with the blade. Literally cutting the very air. Then she looked back at Tako. "Reset your translator, Tako," she ordered him.

After a few moments, Tako replied in a much quieter, and much higher pitched, voice. "Yes, ma'am."

She sighed again, then turned to gesture in Lisa's direction. "Special Deputy Jingcha Tako, this is Lisa Huntress."

"Hello!" Tako's "normal" voice, the voice transmitted via the translator device he'd been given, sounded even more childlike as he greeted the new human. "Can I have a shiny thing like yours?"

The Huntress glanced sharply at the lightsaber blade protruding from the cylinder attached to her right elbow joint, then deactivated it. *Yep*, Chun thought to herself. She could easily envision the bemused expression behind that helmet. Octopussies, and particularly Tako, tended to have that effect on people. "Tako, the Huntress is here to discuss the murder," Chun explained.

Tako burst out with a sudden, anguished whine. "Oh! It was *horrible!* Blood *everywhere!*" The tips of several of his tentacles rose out of the water, waving theatrically like a grief-stricken mourner bewailing the loss of a loved one.

"Knock it off with the fictional references," Chun snapped.

It shouldn't have been possible for the translator to interpret and express the Octopussy's communication as a resigned sigh, but somehow Tako had found a way. "Fine..." he grumbled.

Chun looked back to the Huntress, giving her an encouraging nod. "Okay," she said. "Go ahead and ask him your questions."

"All right..." Despite what an imposing figure she cut, the Huntress sounded almost like a trained thespian actor who, having walked onstage for had been billed as dramatic improvisation, suddenly found herself serving as the straight man for sketch comedy instead. It took her a few moments to remember the correct words for her first question. "Tako," the Huntress began. "Did you know the ambassador?"

"We met six times," Tako answered, slipping his tentacles back into the water now that his portrayal of an anguished mourner was ended. "Ambassador Sashimi checked on me every ten days, to see if I was being treated well."

"One moment," the Huntress said. "Chun? A word." She turned away and stalked several meters away, far enough for a brief, discrete discussion.

Chun followed, doing her best to maintain a straight face as she joined the FIA agent. Who crouched slightly and leaned in, her audio output lowered to a near whisper. "Sashimi?" she asked, her tone almost plaintive.

"Octopussies don't normally have names," Chun whispered back. "He felt he needed one, in order to interact with us."

Behind her helmet's faceplate, the Huntress' expression was unreadable. But Chun could imagine what it looked like. "Did... did he know what that word means?" the Huntress finally asked.

Chun replied, in as professional and sober a tone as she could manage, "he picked the name himself." After a moment, she added, "So did Tako. Tako is Japanese for "octopus.""

"Oh." The FIA agent digested this for a moment, then walked back towards the tank. "Tako, can you tell me what Sashimi was like?" she asked. Chun had to give her credit; the woman was adapting to the situation with flair.

"I have no idea," Tako immediately replied. "I've never eaten sashimi."

There was a long, pregnant pause, before the Huntress rallied and attempted again. "Tako, can you please tell me what *Ambassador* Sashimi was like?"

Tako said nothing, as his tentacles slowly swirled about in the tank.

"He's thinking," Chun told the Huntress. The armored amazon gave the barest incline of her helmet in acknowledgment, waiting for Tako to think of how to respond.

Finally the childish voice spoke, in more somber tones than before. "He knew how important it was to you, that we join the Federation." Tako's tentacles began to swirl at a slightly increased pace, as if growing agitated. "He took the job... *seriously*."

The Huntress stared at the Octopussy. The Chief Jingcha watched the Huntress, staring at the Octopussy. At which point the Huntress reaffirmed the Chief Jingcha's favorable opinion of her. She hadn't needed any prompting to notice the curious emphasis Tako had placed on that last word. "He took the job seriously," she repeated slowly. "Is that unusual?"

The tentacles swirled inside the water, then coiled about the central mass that was Tako's head. His eyes, and the rest of his head, were completely enfolded as if he were hugging himself. Then the tentacles suddenly exploded outward, rising out of the water in a violent gesture that sent gallons of water splashing over both women. Even with his translator reset to that childlike voice, there was a wrathful fury to his words.

"It's *blasphemous!*"

Taco slithered out of the tank, propelling himself across the ground with astonishing speed. One tentacle slipped underneath the others, probing at the underside of his head – where his mouth was, and where Octopussies were able to keep objects secured in the crevices between the bases of their tentacles. A gleaming chunk of metal was hurled in Chun's direction, and then Tako slithered away, headed straight for the docks.

The Huntress' armor glistened and shone even more brightly in the morning light with the water dripping off of it. She glanced down at the metallic object that had been tossed at their feet. "Is that... his badge?" she tentatively asked.

"Yeah," Chun sighed, crouching down to pick it up. She could feel the water dripping down her body, soaking through her wool jacket, as well as the silk of her uniform beneath. She stood back up and slipped the badge into her pocket. "That was him resigning his commission."

"I... I'm sorry," the Huntress stammered. "I didn't mean to cause any trouble..."

"Don't worry about it." Chun waved one hand in a dismissive gesture. "He turns in his badge every week. Sometimes twice a week, if he feels like it."

The FIA agent said nothing for several moments, before asking the obvious question. "Why?"

"Because "cowboy cops" in bad fiction do it all the time," Chun sighed.

"I see." The Huntress stood there, and despite everything that had happened Chun couldn't help but admire her quiet dignity in the face of such absurdity. "He appears to have quite the sense of humor," the Huntress observed.

"They all do," Chun agreed. "I felt it was best for you to experience it for yourself. They're also exceedingly intelligent," she added. "They're not children, even if they seem to act like it at times."

"Hmm." The FIA agent appeared to be ruminating; Chun waited in patient silence for the next question. "Did he mean what he said?" Lisa finally asked. "About it being... blasphemy? To take things seriously?"

"I don't know," Chun admitted. "We're still learning about each other. I don't know if they have anything like a religion. I couldn't begin tell you what the actual concept is, whatever it was that Tako translated as "blasphemous."'" She shrugged, and the movement caused more water to be squeegeed out of her jacket. "Or if they take it any more seriously than they do anything else."

"Hmm. So did he splash us as some sort of reprimand?" the Huntress mused. "Or as a parting gesture? Or... an expression of distress?"

"It's more like a surprise pie in the face," Chun explained helpfully.

Chapter 11

Chun's already high opinion of the FIA agent had rocketed even further upwards, by the time she'd finished changing into dry clothing. The Huntress' habit of wearing her powered armor at all times had proven to be surprisingly practical. While she had required naught but a towel to wipe down the surface of her armor, the Chief Jingcha had found it necessary to exchange her drenched garments for a clean, dry uniform. For that matter, she also considered it necessary (in her professional opinion as the head of the planetary law enforcement agency) to apply a touch of lipstick. After all, there was no sense in risking chapped lips.

If the Huntress noticed her sensible precaution against dry, cracked lips, she made no comment. She merely clutched her armored knees with both arms and hunched in Chun's car as the older woman drove towards their destination. Chun found herself feeling rather tongue tied, at a loss for small talk during the silence of the ride.

Thankfully it was a short trip, given that the Gonganting was located on the coast, much like the hydroelectric plants that provided the majority of the electrical energy consumed by the colony. It was to Wigglebiggle Hydroelectric Plant #3 (formerly Varuna Hydroelectric Plant #3) that they were headed, and soon Chun was parking in the lot outside the facility. After a slight delay for the Huntress to extricate herself from the confines of the vehicle, they were headed in through the front door, walking beneath a sign labeled "VHP-3."

They still haven't changed that, I see.

Director Stuart was waiting for them just inside the door. The Huntress stopped several meters away, looming there before the slender, elderly figure. She said nothing, obviously waiting to be introduced by the Chief Jingcha as an authorized investigator. "Good morning, Artis," Chun greeted them, then waved a hand at her towering companion. "This is the Federation agent we requested. Lisa Huntress, this is Artis Stuart, the director for this plant."

"Hello," the Huntress murmured, before falling silent.

"Hello," Artis replied, with a strained smile on their wizened face. "I'm hoping you can solve things," they added, the stress and tension in their voice unmistakable. "We're all rather tense at the moment." Turning smartly on one heel, the director began to walk away. "If you'll follow me, I'll give you a tour, and answer your questions."

They trailed in Director Stuart's wake, walking past the decidedly odd décor furnishing the walls. The gleaming helmet pivoted as the Huntress observed the tallies of names, hanging from bright red frames. "So how does your facility generate energy?" she inquired, her massive boots landing almost as lightly as their guide's soft rubber soled shoes.

"We actually rely on a combination of methods for power generation," Astrid explained. Their voice grew more steady as the discussion leaned towards their area of expertise. "Diversification is vital, when it comes to vital resources."

"Naturally," agreed the Huntress, as they continued to walk down the halls.

"The first is through underwater tesla turbines," Astrid elaborated, waving a slender fingered hand in gesticulation. "They take in tidal waters, channeling the energy for electromagnetic induction. We also have buoys that float on the surface, rising and falling with the waves. The motion powers a series of pumps for a secondary induction system."

"But all the electricity is generated from the movement of the ocean water, correct?"

Astrid nodded at the Huntress' question. "That's correct. The colony also has a number of wind farms, and many of the buildings have solar panels for additional generation. A diverse set of sources, just in case something goes wrong. And of course this is only one of four hydroelectric plants."

"Do you use any methods that require external fuel sources?" Even as she asked, the Huntress continued to glance at the oddly framed lists on the walls. Bright red plastic frames, shaped like cartoon rabbits. Chun felt a twinge of amusement; she was well aware of how odd they looked at first glance.

"Those are costly and inefficient," the director answered. "As for us, as long as everything's working, the power is created automatically. Our job is just to keep everything working."

"I see."

The Huntress' clipped response made Chun smile, and she turned her head in an attempt to cover up her amused expression. *She's going to ask...*

The Huntress did not disappoint. "So what's with the bunny rabbits?"

Artis looked over their shoulder, and the wrinkles on the wizened face shifted into a web of beaming pride. "That's been my biggest accomplishment, I'd have to say. The Red Rabbit system."

"Huh," the Huntress grunted. "How does it work?"

"It's actually been in use for over a thousand years," the director explained. "Introducing red colored parts into systems, and directing employees to keep a sharp lookout for them. It was first used in factories, for quality control."

"And you're using it in a hydroelectric facility," the Huntress noted.

"You could say we're a factory that manufactures electricity," Astrid quipped. "But more importantly, it's all about warding off the most dangerous threat to our facility. Boredom."

The Huntress stopped walking for a moment, glancing sharply at one of the lists of names. At the top of the list were the words, "Turbine Technician Category." Each name was accompanied by a series of tally marks. "Boredom," she repeated.

"Oh yes," Artis exclaimed. "Maintenance and inspections are among the most important jobs for a technological society. But they're also... well, boring. This job can be boring." They shrugged nonchalantly, admitting the truth of the nature of the job freely and without shame. "And if we get bored, we slack off. If we slack off... things can go wrong, because we're not paying attention."

"So you make the job more fun," the Huntress said. Her voice sounded speculative, yet there was a definite undertone of approval there.

"We use paintball pellets to shoot components in hard to reach places," Astrid said, their wrinkled features crinkling with an impish expression. "Red dyes to pour into the turbines..."

"Red robot rodents?" The cylinder that was the Huntress' right forelimb pointed in the direction of the tiny figure wriggling out from under a doorframe. It quickly ambled towards a vending machine, slipping behind it and out of sight.

"Well done. I should open a category for visitors," Astrid declared appreciatively.

"You divide them up by categories?" As they resumed their tour, the Huntress leaned against the vending machine, attempting to peer behind it for signs of the tiny crimson drone.

"It wouldn't be fair, otherwise." Artis pulled at a door handle, opening the way into a room at which several consoles were being tended to by dutiful looking underlings. "The technicians here spend most of their time sitting around, not roaming the halls like the electricians or the janitors. The janitors don't get to watch the monitors. Different categories makes the game more fair, and thus, fun." They waved a hand in passing greeting to the technicians, calling out to them, "Keep up the good work, people."

A few grunts of acknowledgment and a lone "yes, boss" trailed behind them as the trio moved on to the next room. "I introduced the Red Rabbit contests a few decades ago, and now all four plants emulate our methods," Astrid boasted. "Some of the local industries have begun to adopt similar practices. The fishing industry in particular... oh, right..." The proud boasting faded to an embarrassed murmur.

"With so much attention to detail, you must have found the ambassador's corpse fairly quickly," the Huntress observed. "It was inside one of the turbines, correct?"

Astrid visibly winced. "I... wouldn't call it a corpse. More like... ground meat."

"Hum." Chun gave a sidelong, and upwards, glance, wondering what sort of contemplative expression the face behind that helmet might have at the moment. Then the Huntress quipped, "So it really was a red turbine?"

Behind the wrinkles, Director Stuart's expression grew primly disapproving. "Actually, Octopussy blood is a dark blue. Almost purple." They continued to frown as they added, "but yes, we found it almost immediately. It only took a few seconds to notice the obstruction and shut down the turbine. We sent out a submersible drone within five minutes, and then... well, that's when we called the Gonganting and reported what we'd found."

The rest of the tour was conducted under rather less pleasant conditions, as Astrid attempted to explain some of the technological minutia of the facility. Despite the occasional stream of long, flowing polysyllables cutting through the attempts at a succinct layperson's explanation, the Huntress appeared to be following every word. Until at last she declared, "I think we're done here, for now."

"Very well," Director Stuart acceded. "Are you sure there isn't anything else I can help with?"

"We might have more questions later," the Huntress replied, as they drifted towards the exit, and by extension to Chun's car. "But you've been very helpful."

"I hope you'll find the murderer soon," the director grimaced. "This has been... awful."

"Yes," came the response. Whether in agreement about the awfulness of the situation, or in assurance of her intent to catch her prey, or both.

Chun was prepared to bet money that it was that last option. And to lay down even more money on a swift and successful capture. *It's been amazing, watching her at work. No wonder she's so good at her job.*

Chapter 12

So far, so good. Lisa's scheme to use eccentricity as an excuse to wear her armor was working out thus far. The same industrial grade XTMP-III workhorse that shielded her from temperature extremes, radiation, and physical impacts also served to protect her from social interactions and public exposure. As long as the Chief Jingcha couldn't see her expressions, Lisa felt she had a sufficient advantage that she could endure the woman's aggressive attention and her fake camaraderie. She could only wonder why "nice, friendly Chun" was so focused on investigating her, but being the target of a law enforcement official was rather nerve wracking.

Still, it's not as if she can overpower me. Lisa was armored, protected against the majority of possible attacks or attempts to physically restrain her. She was almost beginning to feel smug about her cleverness, as they walked past a rectangular shaped building after having parked Chun's vehicle.

At which point nice, friendly Chun wiped the smugness away with a simple suggestion. "Let's stop here and get some food," she declared, seemingly on a whim. She veered away from Lisa and towards the large window set in the side of the building, where a young woman sat behind the counter, waiting for passing customers.

"What, here?" Lisa blurted out, instantly realizing the flaw in her scheme. She stumbled after Chun, too upset about the dawning awareness that she wouldn't be able to ***eat*** anything to even notice the frightened look on the pimple dappled face of the girl in the kiosk.

"This is *the* place for Varuna rolls," Chun breathed, while holding up a hand with two fingers extended. "Two rolls, please."

Lisa wanted to cry. The girl was preparing the rolls by hand, no automation necessary for her simple fare. Long rolls were snatched up, one at a time, pulled open along their pre-sliced groove, then tossed onto a griddle to toast. It took only a few seconds for the exterior surfaces of each roll to be left golden and crisped.

Toasted buns. She's toasting the buns. It looked so good. And that was only the start, as the girl ladled the filling into each roll. Whatever it was, it was glistening with a creamy dressing, and looked decidedly chunky, the bite sized pieces of protein nestling in their toasted beds.

Chun held up one to Lisa, and Lisa would have sworn that there was a sadistic tinge to that seemingly friendly little smile. "Here, pop that helmet and take a bite," Chun pressed her. "You've never had anything as good as these."

Lisa felt like crying. Or screaming. She wanted to. She wanted to so badly. It looked so good. But taking her helmet off would ruin the reputation for eccentricity that she was trying so hard to cultivate. But her stomach was beginning to growl, because it had been several hours since she'd eaten her leftovers and called them breakfast, and her body required fuel.

"Not right now, thank you," Lisa managed to choke out.

Her stomach growled again, angrily protesting her decision.

Chun seemed oddly disappointed by the rejection, but took a large bite of the roll and moaned quietly with pleasure. It sounded for all the world as if she were teasing Lisa by savoring the morsel, yet Lisa felt unable to call her out on it. Social convention had her trapped.

Desperate to distract herself, Lisa attempted to engage the girl now sitting placidly behind the counter and watching the happy customer. "So these are... Varuna rolls?" Lisa asked, tentatively probing.

"Yes, zǒng," the girl replied with the professionally polite smile of an experienced worker in a service industry. "My grandfather brought the recipe all the way from Earth. They used to call them "lobster rolls."" She lifted a hand wrapped in a translucent plastic glove and jerked a thumb over her shoulder. "Of course, we use a native species. The Varuna lobster. Grandfather always said they tasted even better than a Maine lobster."

Lisa considered that for a moment. "Maine... a province on Earth?"

"Yes, zǒng," the girl agreed. "We've been serving Varuna lobsters for three generations." She paused for a moment, then the brown skin around her pimples reddened slightly as she shyly added, "I'm the third generation. The second generation's working in the back. My folks."

"I see." Lisa looked over the girl's shoulder, at a doorway leading to the rest of the building. The kiosk itself was rather on the smallish side, taking up only a portion of the building's interior. "So how many do you sell?" she asked politely, trying to distract herself from the furious tantrum her stomach was throwing. Her tongue and palate were beginning to join in;

she swallowed to clear her mouth of the rush of saliva. Her mouth was literally watering!

"Not as many as I'd like to," the girl shrugged. She glanced at Chun, and her expression grew wary, even closed. "Our supplies are limited, because we respect the fishing ban."

Fishing ban? Respect the fishing ban?

That was an interesting statement to make. Somewhat cryptic, especially in the presence of a law enforcement official. *Did I just find my first real clue?* There was definitely something going on there. "What is she talking about?" she asked, turning to look at Chun.

She immediately regretted it. The woman had just popped the last of her first roll into her mouth, and was chewing with obvious delight. In her belly, Lisa's stomach was threatening a general mutiny, and her mouth was letting her know it would be a populist uprising rather than an elitist coup. *I want those rolls. I want them so badly.*

Finally, Chun swallowed and took a breath in order to explain. "This world belongs to the Octopussies. That includes the oceans – and the sea life. We don't want to run the risk of driving their food sources to extinction."

"Right. That was a problem in ancient history," Lisa agreed. "Empires would even do it on purpose, as a method of genocide." She tried to remember some of the examples cited in her history lessons. *North America, and the hunting of the bison. India and the exportation of grain seed. Ireland and the potato famine.* The bison were an especially striking example; the colonists of the planet Lonestar, where Lisa's mentor and adoptive father had retired with his lovers, had deliberately cultivated a recreation of an idealized historical period, and a millennia later the bison roamed the plains of a thoroughly terraformed planet, alongside deer, antelope, and tame herds of taurine cattle.

The thought of how close the bison had come to extinction was outright disturbing, to someone who had come to appreciate the taste of their flesh. *One more example of the evils of colonialism.* Small wonder that the people of Wigglebiggle were so determined to avoid repeating the mistakes of the past.

*Well... perhaps not **all** the people.* Lisa looked back to the pimple faced girl. "So where do you get your lobsters?" she asked.

"We raise them," the girl repeated. "Mom and Dad tend the aquariums in the back. I work the counter. We are respecting... the... ban..." she carefully enunciated, glancing warily at the senior-most law enforcement authority on the planet. Who was currently wolfing down her second Varuna roll.

Lisa could see how uncomfortable the girl was. It made her feel pangs of sympathy to accompany her pangs of hunger. "If you have to raise them yourselves, why not raise Maine lobsters?" she suggested.

The girl shook her head, as her smile grew slightly more... fixed. "That would make them lobster rolls," she demurred. "Not Varuna rolls. You have to use Varuna lobster to make a proper Varuna roll."

"Huh." Lisa frowned thoughtfully and attempted to consider the girl's argument. Her own culinary expertise, aside from her now somewhat hazily remembered times holding food skewered on sticks before the roaring fires of the tribal hearth, was mostly limited to the operation of intelligent kitchen devices. Nonetheless, she could respect a professional's artistic pride. "So are they still Varuna rolls?" she mused, glancing away in the direction of the shoreline. "Or are they Wigglebiggle rolls now?"

"They're *Varuna* rolls," snapped the girl with sudden heat.

Lisa turned back to her, startled by the unexpected vehemence. Next to her, Chun swallowed a bite in silence, and Lisa was surprised to see the authoritative older woman carefully looking away from the angry young woman.

Then Lisa saw why Chun was avoiding meeting the girl's gaze. The girl was glaring directly at the Chief Jingcha, her expression openly challenging. "You can make us call the planet... *Wigglebiggle*, but you can't take this from us!" she seethed, her professional demeanor slipping.

Inside the confines of the building behind her, there was the sound of something heavy being dropped. Lisa felt her hackles raise with immediate wariness, her cripplingly hypersensitive paranoia alerting her to possible danger. Chun paused in the act of chewing, responding to Lisa's subtle shift in body language even through the armor.

A door burst open. The woman charging through it looked to be a similar age to Chun, and her features were tense with worry and anger. "Jing! Go help your father!" she shouted at the pimple faced girl. One work-roughened hand pointed imperiously at the open door.

"They're Varuna rolls!" the girl shot back, even as she hopped off the stool and glared angrily at Chun. *But not at her mother*, Lisa couldn't help but observe. "They'll always be Varuna rolls!" she screamed in defiance, before fleeing through the door and towards where her father was no doubt tending to the lobsters.

Once she'd confirmed her daughter was obeying her directive, the woman turned back to bow in the direction of her customers. "I apologize for my daughter's rudeness," she murmured, her gaze lowered to the point that she must have had a fine view of her own feet.

"She's just upset. It's okay, Chou-fen," Chun replied, offering her a reassuring smile. The woman flushed and shook her head dismissively. Chun sighed and bit her lip, before adding, "anyway, tell Jing I said thanks for the Varuna rolls."

"I will, Bogbum," Jing's mother replied, bowing again. This won a tired, friendly smile from the Chief Jingcha, before she turned to gaze at Lisa, taking another bite of her last roll and waiting patiently.

"I think I've taken up enough of your time for today," Lisa suggested. "You probably have a lot of other things to take care of," she added helpfully.

"Don't I know it," Chun sighed, shaking her head wearily. "But this takes precedence. If you need me for anything, just let me know." After a brief pause, she added, "anything at all."

"Right. Thanks," Lisa said, briefly wondering what had happened to cause the older woman to be so determined to keep an eye on her. *Maybe my rep's even worse than I thought?* It was a sobering concern. But she had other, more pressing concerns, and as soon as Chief Jingcha Callan had walked away sufficiently that Lisa felt safe to speak up, she turned sharply to face Jing's mother, who had taken up her daughter's post atop the stool. "Uh... Chou-fen..." she said in as soft and polite a voice as she could manage.

"It's McCormick Nushi, to you," the woman snapped curtly, frowning up at Lisa's helmeted visage with a fearless glare.

Lisa froze, sensing she'd erred somehow. "Oh... uh... I'm sorry, the Chief Jingcha..."

"Won't stop making fun of me for farting when we were ten," McCormick clarified.

"Oh." Lisa felt the urge to run away and find someplace to curl up and hide, after the social gaffe. "So... that's why you called her..."

"Bogbum, yes. You probably shouldn't call her that,"

McCormick advised. She arched a brow, still glaring up at Lisa. "Did you need something?"

"As a matter of fact... yes," Lisa admitted. She felt the pressing urgency, a desperate need to stave off the general revolt coming from the depths of her empty torso. "Six Varuna rolls. In a bag, or whatever you have for takeout."

McCormick raised the other brow, silently staring up at her.

"Please?" Lisa begged.

Chapter 13

The first thing Lisa did after returning to her room at the Gonganting was to – carefully – set down the bag containing her Varuna rolls, upon the small but perfectly functional desk. The second thing she did was to hastily exit her armor. The third was *not* plugging in the charge; she was too hungry to remember to do so, as she sank down into the chair and pulled out one of the rolls, before tearing the plastic wrapping apart.

The first bite was even more exquisite than she could have hoped, though she couldn't take her time to savor it as much as she might have wanted to. She chewed with a swift fury before swallowing, then took a second ravenous bite. She finally managed to slow herself down enough to better appreciate the third bite, to contemplate the unique flavor. There was definitely some sort of egg based dressing holding everything together, with vinegar and mustard in it. Whatever it was, it added to the richness of the flaky, buttery flavored flesh. The bread, golden crisped on the outside and soft on the inside, was bringing its own notes of deliciousness to the party – the deep, steady back beat of carbohydrates joining the harmony of the proteins and fats. Under the serenade of the Varuna roll, Lisa's stomach, tongue, and palate gradually began to offer a grudging acceptance of her apology.

Once she'd finished the first roll, Lisa could finally *think* again. Which meant it was time to do so. She frowned as she contemplated the situation. After everything she had done so far this day, it was time to reflect and consider the next course of action. It didn't take long for the epiphany to hit with blinding clarity. *Yes.* There was no denying it. There was an incontrovertible fact that she would simply have to face.

I have no idea what I'm doing.

She was no detective! She had just spent the entire morning interviewing potential suspects. Or had she? Was the Octopussy cop a suspect? Was Director Stuart? For that matter, was the pimple faced girl who'd been screaming about the name of her food a suspect? How was she supposed to narrow down the list of possible suspects? Lisa had only the barest understanding of what a suspect even *was!* How was she supposed to figure out who had shoved the Ambassador's body into the turbine?

She had to look at the clues. *What clues do I have?* She only had questions. Such as who the Ambassador even spoke to. Or for that matter, how many Octopussies aside from Tako and Sashimi even interacted with humans. If the killer was an Octopussy, would she *ever* be able to track them down?

Sheer frustration led her to make the call. As much as the Chief Jingcha unnerved her, Lisa needed the woman's help. Even if the prompt acceptance of the call reaffirmed Lisa's suspicions. *This woman is investigating **me**.*

Lisa would simply have to add the question of "why?" to the list of things she needed to find an answer to. "Has Tako come back for his badge yet?" she asked.

"Not yet," Callan replied. "He's usually gone for a day or

two, before he comes back. I'm pretty sure it's all an excuse to go home and spend time with his own kind – I mean, his own people," she hastily corrected herself.

"Good at slipping through gaps in the system," Lisa sighed, before clenching her mouth shut to avoid saying anything else that might be construed as insensitive or bigoted. *Do **not** say anything **else** about invertebrates being good at slithering through cracks.*

Thankfully, Callan gave a wry chuckle at the bad joke. "He'll be back. He can't watch his shows in the ocean."

"Yes, what sort of..." Lisa paused, her forehead furrowing as she attempted to remember the term, "..."cowboy cop" shows does he watch?"

"Oh, he likes everything," the Chief Jingcha chuckled again, this time with an affectionate tone as she revealed this bit of personal information about one of her more unusual subordinates. "He's voracious for stories. Apparently telling stories is a huge part of Octopussy culture."

"So... maybe he keeps going home to tell the other Octopussies about the shows he's been watching?" Lisa suggested.

There was a brief pause. "That... might actually be it," Callan reflected. "They're *really* into stories."

Interesting. And possibly a clue. If not about the murder, then at least about their culture. "So what sort of shows does he watch?" Lisa repeated her previous question.

"Like I said, a variety," Callan echoed. "We can always tell when he's started watching something new, because he starts imitating whatever he sees."

Interesting. And... a clue? "So what sort of shows did he watch, before he started throwing away his badge?" Lisa wondered.

Callan made a disgusted noise. "*Dirty Harry*," she spat the name. "It's a 28th century remake of an obscure film from the Dark Times..."

"You let him look at Dark Times material!?"

If Callan flinched at Lisa's horrified outcry, the audio-only conversation provided no hint of it. "Patrick – I mean, the Governor – insisted on allowing full access to all of our records."

Lisa said nothing, mutely horrified by the idea of 20th century media contaminating a pure and innocent alien culture. Polluting a pristine society with the taint of Fey influence.

"I happen to agree with him," Callan added, sounding defensive about it. "If we held anything back, they could accuse us of being duplicitous. They needed to learn about us, including the ugly parts of us."

Lisa shook her head slightly in horrified disbelief. "And... you just let him watch?"

"No, we provided context on what he was seeing," Callan retorted, heatedly defending her actions. "We made it clear that he was watching behaviors we shun today. Then I gave him some of my favorite shows to watch."

Is this going to be a clue as well? "What sort of shows did you give him to watch?" Lisa asked.

"Andy." Now Callan sounded pleased with herself. Or possibly just pleased at the mention of the show.

"What's "Andy" about?" Lisa inquired.

The older woman definitely sounded happy to discuss it. "It came out three years ago, and it's still going. I watch the new episodes as soon as they're out."

"Okay..." Lisa said slowly. "But what's it about?"

"It's an ancient Earth collection of stories about a legendary fictional law enforcement official," Callan positively purred, with an excitement that Lisa belatedly realized was the giddiness of a true fan. "Tako's also watched the older versions, but when the new episodes come on, he'll watch it with me and some of my other people. Unless he's "quit the force" that day," she added.

"Is this produced... locally?" Lisa wondered.

"No, it's shot on Earth. New Hollywood."

"Oh." Lisa suppressed a slight shudder, unpleasant memories of her – thankfully – brief time in New Hollywood flashing through her mind. "But it's a fictional character, right?" she asked. "Does he know the difference between fiction and history?"

"Amazingly well," the Chief Jingcha admitted. "I suppose, since he's a sapient being, he understands deception and lying. And that's what fiction is, in a sense. Stories that are lies?"

"Yeah," Lisa agreed. "So what else has he watched?"

"Um... a bit of everything, really." Callan sounded as if she were floundering to give an answer. "Shows for children. Shows for adults. Comedies. Dramas. Oh!" she grunted. "If it helps, I think he was watching a Sherlock Holmes show, the week before the murder happened."

"All right," Lisa acknowledged. Then she asked, "Who's Sherlock Holmes?"

"Huh? Oh, right," Callan grunted a grimace of apology. "He's another ancient Earth legend, like Robin Hood or Guan Yu."

Lisa had heard the occasional vague allusion to Robin Hood once or twice over the years, but neither name carried any recognition with her. But Callan had mentioned it, as if it were important. Was it? "Is... Sherlock Holmes a killer, or something?" she wondered aloud.

"Heh. No," Callan chuckled at the naivety of the question. "But he catches a fair share of killers. He's a detective, like you."

Not like me. Not if he were even remotely competent at what he did. Whoever Sherlock Holmes had been, real or fictional, his stories no doubt involved him being more thoroughly capable at the job of solving mysteries than a bounty hunter like herself. The thought rushed through her mind, of a charismatic gentleman in antiquated garb, casually putting together the clues, doing everything that Lisa herself lacked the training, experience, or competence to do.

That thought was followed by a sudden burst of inspiration.

"Is there anything else I can help you with?" Callan asked, the silence having stretched on a little too long.

"I think... you might have just helped me plenty," Lisa breathed.

"Are you sure?" the woman repeated herself. Pushy and determined to keep an eye on Lisa, for whatever twisted reason she had.

"I'm very sure, yes," Lisa reiterated, though she was feeling too elated to feel particularly defensive at that moment. "I... I'll call you if I need anything. But for now... I... I've got things to work on," she trailed off, glancing downward almost demurely – even though it was an audio-only conversation.

Once she'd ended the call, Lisa continued to stare down at the desk. At the bag. Then she withdrew a second roll, tearing the plastic wrapping away. She felt like eating it at the desk, before relocating to the bed. There was a large viewscreen against the wall opposite the head of the bed, and Lisa had little doubt that it was meant for entertainment more than professional work. These were residential quarters for unmarried cops, for Jingcha, and viewscreens in bedrooms were traditional on most worlds.

She didn't even bother to finish the second roll, before taking both it and the bag containing the last four of its companions to the bed. Perhaps she didn't know what to do, but if someone else did, then she had the perfect role model to study. Settling into a comfortable position, Lisa began to scroll through the menu in search of shows about... *Sherlock Holmes*.

Chapter 14

Whenever Patrick needed to interrupt someone during their work hours, he brought food with him. It wasn't even about winning reelection; local custom dictated that he stayed in office until someone challenged him, and only then did everyone put it to a vote. Since nobody seemed to want the job (and lately there had been days when he'd happily abdicate in favor of anyone who did), he was stuck. But his mother had taught him from an early age that good food made bad news go down a little more smoothly.

Especially when it was Chun. The Chief Jingcha would of course never, ever dream of roughing up a suspect (particularly since their criminal element consisted of fishermen who liked to get rowdy when they'd been drinking, a couple of smugglers, and an old man with a penchant for streaking). But it was another story when it came to expressing her annoyance with her putative superior. Especially a superior she'd grown up with. Patrick didn't feel like being on the receiving end of a frustrated tirade. More importantly, he knew about her love of shortbreads.

Before dropping by to check for updates regarding the

crisis that might very well result in the end of the colony and their way of life, Patrick made certain to bring an especially large and diverse assortment from Mary's Bake'ry. Only after she'd opened the box to behold the variety of expensive pastries did Patrick ask how the investigation was going.

"Badly," Chun mumbled through a mouthful of chocolate, caramel, and shortbread.

Patrick poured a dollop of milk into his coffee to accompany the sugar, stirring in silence as he waited for her to elaborate. When no such elaboration was forthcoming, he took a sip before sighing. "So where's that amazing "Huntress" of yours?"

"In her room," Chun sighed, with a weary shake of her head. "She's been staying in her room this whole time."

Patrick's forehead furrowed in a puzzled frown. "It's been three days," he couldn't help but note. "Are you sure she's...?" He trailed off rather than finish the question, *still alive?*

"She came out once or twice to make a few purchases," Chun conceded, giving the shortbread in her hand a melancholy glower. "Food, mostly."

"What, you haven't gone out for a dinner date yet?" Patrick couldn't help himself. Nor could he help flinching under the murderous glare Chun shot at him.

Fortunately Chun was able to help herself. Rather than throw the chunk of shortbread at his head, she instead opted to shovel the confection into her mouth, chewing with gusto as if venting her anger upon it. "She doesn't even talk to anyone," she seethed. "She just comes out – always in that damned armor – then comes back with about ten kilos of takeout and shuts the door. I have no idea what she's doing."

"Sampling the local cuisine?" Patrick mused. He followed suit, reaching for a piece of shortbread that he hoped wouldn't be too sorely missed.

They consumed the shortbread together in relative harmony, Patrick discretely changing the subject to inquire about Chun's nephews. Fortunately there was some good news there, and Chun gratefully boasted about Jet taking fourth place in the school poetry competition. Patrick wouldn't have known what to do if the kid had bombed.

They were down to just a handful of the salted shortbread pieces (the ones coated with salt – but not chocolate – being both his least favorite, and Chun's) by the time the giant armored figure strode into the office. "Ah, she emerges," Patrick couldn't help but quip.

The looming form froze, turning slightly to face him. Patrick felt the blood drain from his face as a sudden wave of trepidation hit. She glared at him in silence for a few brief, terrifying moments, before speaking. "I apologize," the Huntress' deep, husky voice rumbled. "I've been doing some important research."

"I see," Chun murmured, looking cowed and shy in the other woman's presence.

Patrick knew better than to think that Chun felt intimidated or threatened. *She's still not over her crush.* Aloud, he spoke up, "I hope you found something."

The Huntress' helmet swiveled slightly, glancing towards the Chief Jingcha, then back towards the Governor. "So do I. It was very important research." She fell silent for a moment, then added, "critical. I am now ready to begin interviewing people."

"All right," Chun nodded. "I'm very busy at the moment, but I should be able to escort you in an hour."

"...Oh." The Huntress fell silent after the faint grunt of surprised acknowledgment. She glanced back at Chun, then back at Patrick. Then back at Chun again, as if confused. In that gleaming armor, she looked not unlike a bipedal drone with a crashed operating system.

Patrick heard his own throat being cleared. "I could drive you around, if you like," he offered, before his conscious mind could catch up to his reflexive urges to accommodate others and put them at their ease.

"I... would like that, yes," the Huntress replied. Suddenly Patrick found himself wondering how old the woman actually was. Even with the slight distortion of the armor's audio output, she sounded like a shy teenager.

It was... puzzling. *Is she some sort of savant?* But her record spoke for itself. And Patrick trusted Chun's judgment. If Chun thought this woman could help them, then this woman could help them. "Right. I guess you'll be riding in the back again?" he asked, stepping around the armored woman and out the door.

"Yes. Thank you," the Huntress agreed, as she moved to follow.

Chapter 15

When you eliminate the impossible, whatever remains, no matter how improbable, must be the truth. Lisa had spent the last few days engaged in relentless study of the methodology of investigative sleuthing, as demonstrated by the fictional character whose earliest stories possibly predated the Fey infiltration. Of course she'd also scoured the ultranet for nonfictional resources, particularly written articles. Articles on the techniques and methods employed by investigators, to be read while videos played in the background. For days she had aggressively consumed the details of how investigators had plied their craft through the centuries.

She had also been forced to discount and dismiss any number of potentially useful techniques, based on the circumstances of her particular situation; fingerprints and DNA analysis were both useless when it came to alien bodies found stuffed into a turbine and chopped into minced calamari. Or owing to the evolution of technology through the centuries; a 25th century version of Detective Holmes might have relied on the cybernetic skills of her Doctor Watson in restoring the deleted memories of a witness' uploaded mind, but Wigglebiggle lacked the transhumanist culture of the planet known as Matrix. *And nobody actually goes there anymore. Or leaves it.* Lisa shuddered faintly at the very thought of that benighted world, with its inhabitants now emaciated corpses locked into the chambers that had turned human beings – willing human beings, granted – into something very like artificial intelligences.

Then of course there were the techniques that had to be discounted on the grounds of being impossible, ungrounded in reality. Such as the 22nd century Holmes who would take two dimensional pictures with his commlink, then rotate them around, zoom into the background to capture minute details, and otherwise perform feats that wouldn't have been feasible even with multiple cameras providing data for a three dimensional simulation.

Or the techniques that were simply *beyond* her; Lisa supposed that Shere Lock Home might have been able to casually look a subject over and swiftly discern their profession, their romantic history, favorite hobbies, and what they ate for dinner the previous evening, but Lisa herself lacked the ability to cross-index minute details against a digital encyclopedia in real time. Or even to replicate the "classic" Holmes' ability to do so with naught but his own command of trivia in 19th century England.

But there were also a dizzying array of video games, and the previous evening, while nibbling on boiled eggs and attempting to solve the Mystery of the Silversmith's Skull, Lisa had finally achieved an epiphany. All the methodology – forensics, interrogation, surveillance, undercover work – were nothing more than methods of obtaining useful data. Clues. Whether Holmes was examining fingerprints through his magnifying glass or disguising herself as a crippled war veteran turned human trafficker, the common element was how they used the available data to narrow down the range of possibilities.

That morning Lisa had focused on rice, fried eggs, chicken legs, and the crime scene itself. Whoever had killed the ambassador would have either stuffed the corpse into the turbine, or else had an accomplice to do so. *Which means... if I can find out who could have done that, I'll have my list of suspects.* She had already discounted the possibility of the killer being a fellow Octopussy on the grounds that, had it been another Octopussy, it was more than likely that they would have already caught the culprit within their own ranks.

It was a very good rationalization, and it allowed her to avoid dwelling on her other reason for ignoring an entire species' worth of potential suspects. Namely, that she would have given up and admitted failure rather than face such a daunting task.

Besides, Wigglebiggle needs a human killer, to show that they hold their own accountable.

Lisa felt the vehicle slowing to a halt, and jerked herself from her reverie as they reached their destination. Before the Governor could exit the cab, she had already hopped out of the bed of his truck. She felt this shouldn't be too strenuous on her; she had already met with Director Stuart once, and now the sheer dread of broaching a stranger in intense conversation had been supplanted by the mere trepidation of interrogating a casual acquaintance she had already met.

There was a small object just inside the front doors, its fluffy red little body waiting in the middle of the hallway. As soon as Lisa caught sight of it the diminutive drone turned and scampered off with impressive speed. Lisa powered after the thing, with the Governor giving a surprised yelp before he rushed to follow.

Down the hall the drone streaked, slipping under the crack beneath the door to what proved to be an office. Director Stuart's office, to be precise. The wizened face shifted into a cobweb of lines as they smiled with pleased amusement. "That's another point for you."

"Does it count if you program them to serve as tour guides?" Lisa asked, coming to a stop with her arm stretched outwards, holding the door for Patrick.

"With some of the new hires, we make it especially easy to spot the red rabbits. At least to begin with," Stuart added, even as they wriggled a few fingers at the little drone. The mechanical rodent skittered away, slipping out of the room and away on whatever route had been selected for it. "Once they get better at spotting them, we let them compete at the same difficulty levels as their colleagues."

Lisa ignored the departing drone, choosing instead to focus on the director. "I need whatever recordings you can give me from your external cameras," she said without further preamble, by way of explanation for her return visit.

"Ah." The patchwork of wrinkles on Director Stuart's face shifted as the amused smile gave way to an apologetic frown. "I'm afraid we don't have any external cameras," they explained.

Lisa froze in position, staring at nothing as her plan to reduce the number of potential suspects down to a manageable amount began to implode on her.

"We've never had a need for external cameras," Stuart went on. "The buoys are brightly marked, so people know to keep a safe distance."

"You're not worried about them approaching the buoys on

purpose?" Lisa asked, trying not to sound as if she were pleading. *Please, let me get a different answer!*

"Not unless they want to risk damaging their craft. And the criminal charges for damaging the buoys," Stuart replied.

Damaging the buoys... "What about deliberate sabotage?" Lisa asked, grabbing for any possible thread.

Stuart's wrinkled face scrunched up in bemused horror. "Who would even do such a thing?" they wondered aloud, visibly disturbed by the very suggestion.

In the back of Lisa's mind a voice reminded her that sometimes Sherlock Holmes had to discomfit potential witnesses in order to get at the truth about the case. But another, louder voice was recriminating her for distressing a respected official of advanced years and indeterminate gender. A Sherlock Holmes might have explained exactly who would do such a thing before repeating the question, but a Lisa Huntress opted to instead change the line of questioning. "Does anyone come near the plant for more... conventional reasons?"

"Well..." Stuart considered the question for several long moments, as the *well* hung in the air. "We used to have fishermen sailing past, but that was before the fishing ban. Months ago."

Damn it. Her most important question, derailed. She was back to an entire colony's worth of suspects!

No, wait. The fishing ban. This was the second time that someone had mentioned the ban on fishing. And the last time, it had sounded as if there were some very hard feelings about it. *An economic motive.* It wouldn't be the first time someone had killed an individual standing between them and a profit.

"Huntress?"

Lisa suddenly became aware that Stuart was speaking.

"Hmm?" she murmured, flinching slightly. The armor must have amplified the movement to a startling degree, because the director shrank back in her chair. "Sorry!" she yelped. "I was... thinking. To myself."

"Ah. I quite understand." Stuart managed a weak smile in acceptance of the apology. "Did you have any further questions?"

"Not at this time, no," Lisa replied, before turning to leave. Then she paused, as her desperate desire to be liked – *or at least, not feared and hated* – compelled her to add, "you may have given me a lead after all. Thank you very much."

Director Stuart nodded their head, smiling in tolerant acceptance.

"And... sorry. For scaring you," Lisa added, trying to feel more like a professional detective, and less like a naughty child, as she departed/fled the hydroelectric plant.

She was already climbing into the bed of the truck by the time Patrick caught up to her. "So where are we headed to next?" he asked, his voice sounding so... neutral. As if he were skeptical of her abilities.

Great. That's all I need. It would be only a matter of time, at this rate, before she was revealed as a complete and utter fraud. *But hopefully not before I've solved the case.* Never mind for her own sake; this colony needed her to succeed if it was going to survive.

All these people are depending on me...

"I'd like to talk to some of the fishermen, next," Lisa told him, struggling to keep her voice sounding confident and steady.

Stuart reached out to grip the handle for the door of his truck's cab, as his forehead furrowed. "I just hope some of them are still sober," he sighed, sounding unenthusiastic about the prospect.

Sober? Lisa glanced upwards at the sky. The sun was still rising into the air, brightly illuminating the atmosphere with its own unique shade of blue. Every world's coloration was dependent upon the atmospheric composition, each one uniquely lovely. "It's your world's mid-morning," she pointed out.

The governor responded with a weary groan. "That late? Then they're definitely drunk by now."

Chapter 16

Archie Wang was on his second buttery when the mercenary walked in. He might have been more annoyed about that if he were still on his first; government thugs and lackeys tended to ruin his appetite. But each buttery was accompanied by several hundred grams of smoked fish and three whiskeys, and he was feeling just buzzed enough to appreciate the entertainment.

The mercenary was undoubtedly on the large side, even without the suit. Archie recognized the general model, something from the XTMP series. They were great for working under all sorts of hazardous conditions, from the vacuum of space to the crushing pressure of deep sea work. The first colonists had brought a few hundred XTMPs of various models with them, an assemblage of used workhorses from secondhand dealers offering equipment for colonists on a budget. Most of them were still in working order today, Voruna's militia arsenal finding far more use in construction and engineering projects than in defending against any theoretical invading armadas. Not that they would be even slightly less effectual under combat conditions; "military grade" traditionally meant "supplied by the lowest bidder," whereas "industrial grade" meant "engineered to withstand conditions far in excess of its official rating, in a pinch."

Still, it was clearly a mercenary in that suit, not a construction worker. For starters, it was lacking the bright yellow paint job, ensuring clear visibility, of the Voruna suits. Not to mention the modifications to one of the limbs. Whatever was up with that cylinder jutting out from where a forearm ought to be, it was decidedly less useful than two good hands, for most jobs. Besides, there was just something about the figure, the way it carried itself, that implied nervous hostility.

Or perhaps Archie was just drunk and jumping to conclusions. Either way, he was looking forward to having some fun.

Nor was he alone in that sentiment. "Are we being invaded?" Finfan inquired in a mild tone, glancing up from his plate of bao.

The mercenary's helmet whipped around sharply, intense focus being brought to bear upon Archie's friend. Archie's friend took another bite from the bun in his hand, chewing calmly as he regarded the armored figure looming before him with casual interest.

Seconds passed, as Finfan chewed, swallowed. Took another bite. Resumed chewing, while he and Archie watched the tall, looming figure to see what it would do next.

Finally, the armored figure spoke. "Is anyone here a fisherman?" came the deep, husky voice from the helmet's audio output.

"None of us are," Archie declared, lifting his glass in a toast to their new playmate. "Fishing's against the law, after all!"

The mercenary turned to stare at Archie. Archie knocked

back the glass, downing the whiskey in one smooth, practiced swallow. The glass was slammed down against the table, clacking loudly as he set it down so roughly, even as he watched to see what would come next.

What came next was a slightly pained tone. "Who here was a fisherman... *before* the fishing ban?" the mercenary clarified.

Archie lifted his hand as if a teacher were calling to students in class. So did Finfan. So did most of the other patrons. Some were already too drunk to follow the conversation. *Lightweights.*

The armored figure, whoever they were, continued to focus their attention upon Archie. "How do you feel about the ban?" the mercenary asked.

Archie glanced at Finfan, who took another bite of steamed bun, chewing nonchalantly as he let Archie field the question. Then Archie looked back at the mercenary, his face splitting into a broad grin. "Why, I just love it!" he loudly declared. "I just love getting to sit on my ass, eating butteries, instead of having to go out and work for a living!"

The armored figure hesitated, then turned to face the pub entrance. Archie looked to see what the mercenary was looking at, and felt his eyebrows climb with interest. *Is that old Glakit Patrick?*

It certainly seemed to be. "Are the fishermen being compensated?" the mercenary asked of the governor.

"Yeah," Archie answered on behalf of Glakit Patrick. "I'm getting paid to sit around while barnacles grow on my boat's hull."

The helmet swiveled back to stare at him in silence for several long moments. Then, in a slightly confused voice, the merc asked, "are you... really okay, with the fishing ban?"

Archie stared back at the helmet's visage, the disbelief almost sufficient to sober him up.

"You're kind of an idiot, aren't you?" Finfan chimed in, a sausage clutched in his fist. He'd finished his bao, and had now moved on to the bangers.

The armored mercenary whipped about, glaring threateningly at Finfan – and Archie almost felt sorry for the government thug. It had all the makings of a terrifying pose, to be sure. The explosive movement. The stature, the bulk, the undeniable anger evident in the posture. That sort of thing might have been rather effective against a landsman. Not so much against someone who'd faced a fifty meter tall rogue wave in pursuit of a catch. For someone like Finfan, a little thug in a metal suit wasn't quite as intimidating as the ocean deciding to go vertical without warning. Finfan bit down on his sausage, chewing noisily as he nonchalantly returned the stare.

That left Archie to do the speaking. "I've been going out on my grandfather's boat since I was old enough to walk," he spoke. "Never gone more than a few days on land until the pì yòng fishing ban, because the fish don't belong to us, according to Glakit Patrick over there."

The governor flushed and swallowed, but made no attempt to draw closer from his position just inside the door. A perfect location from which to run away. Archie sneered at the pathetic coward, then reached for his glass. The realization that he'd already finished the drink only served to further infuriate him, and he snapped, "Now I'm stuck in a pub... because a bunch of bái chī bastards, who've never even been to Varuna, say I'm not really a native to *my* home planet!"

The mercenary stared at Archie in silence, as if watching

to see if Archie were about to initiate violence. Archie stared back, waiting for the excuse to initiate violence. *Just give me a reason, you canned hash. I'll open you up like a tin of corned beef.* His fingers were already twitching reflexively, curling and uncurling as he contemplated hitting Patrick's thug with a chair until the helmet came off.

Finally, the thug spoke. "Do you hate the Octopussies?"

"Do you think we're as stupid as you are, shǎ bī?" Finfan cut in, before Archie could deliver his own, similar answer. Neither of them was about to admit to hating the "indigenous population." Nobody in the pub was stupid enough to admit to hating the "indigenous population."

Oh no. We're not falling for that one. Archie was drunk, but it'd take at least two more butteries – with the attendant three drinks apiece – before he'd fall for such an obvious setup.

Then he belatedly realized what Finfan had just called the thug. *Shǎ bī?* "How can you tell?" Archie asked his friend, both surprised and impressed at Finfan's powers of perception.

Finfan smirked, his eyes roaming over the woman's armored form as if it were translucent. "I can spot a fine arse no matter what it's covered in," he boasted, waggling his eyebrows suggestively.

Glakit Patrick's thug of a shǎ bī stared at Finfan. Then she glanced down at the cylinder where her right hand ought to have been. Then back at Finfan. Then she turned, walking out of the pub with the stiff gait of a mortally offended woman who dared not actually engage in violence.

Finfan whistled appreciatively – and loudly – at her retreating posterior. Archie chuckled and nodded in agreement. That big cow might have been some kind of idiot, but at least her gait, even through her armor, definitely looked feminine to eyes whose perception was most assuredly enhanced by six shots of whiskey.

"Ride that ass some time," Archie muttered to himself, then waved to Simlee, behind the bar, to bring him another buttery with smokies and shots.

Chapter 17

Lisa stared out at the waterfront, busily focused on her breathing. Deep, slow breaths, to slow her heart rate and calm her mind. Her mind badly needed the calming. She had entered the pub feeling nervous, with her usual fear of social interactions. She had exited the pub with the sense that her fears had been validated, to say nothing of the frustration and helpless rage at men whom she could not use violence against. At least, not without serious consequences vastly exceeding the present frustration.

Intellectually she understood that. Not that it lessened her desire to reenter the pub and toss the fishermen around like disposable containers. Her anger remained, even as she breathed. *Deep breaths.* But the anger was demanding physical action, the pent up emotional energy was calling for a release, and... and...

And the Governor is watching.

The awareness that she was being watched worked where mere breathing could not. She was still desperate to retain his good opinion, even if she was also fearfully certain that she'd already lost it. And she had been silent for several minutes at this point, and he was waiting for her to say something.

"I... I didn't handle that very well," she muttered. "Did I." It wasn't a question.

"Eh," Patrick replied in a dismissive fashion, his shoulders heaving in a laconic shrug. "There's no good way to handle drunk fishermen." He sniffed delicately, then added, "but at least you didn't hurt anyone. So... there's that, anyway."

There wasn't much Lisa could think of to say in response to that. She felt utterly wretched about it. This had been her only real lead, and she'd completely bungled it. And the entire colony was depending on her to solve the case, and *the case was proving to be unsolvable...*

Then it occurred to her to wonder aloud, "wait... who's paying for them to sit around and drink?"

Patrick gave her an answer. "The Wigglebiggle government is compensating them for the duration. It's only fair, since we're not letting them work."

Lisa turned to look at the Governor. Patrick had his hands in the pockets of his pants, looking rather nonchalant about everything. Was he hiding his disappointment in her? Did he still think she had a chance of solving the case? He seemed calm enough about all of this.

"It probably does help a bit, not having to worry about where their next meal is coming from," she reflected.

"There's a lot we can learn from the Dark Times," Patrick observed. "About what *not* to do. Forcibly depriving citizens without compensation is near the top of the list, for folks doing a job like mine."

Lisa blinked in bemusement, though of course her helmet obscured it as readily as it did all of her other expressions and reactions. "That... that was a thing?" she blurted out. A sudden reminder that she was supposed to be "the Dark

Times expert" hit her, and she added hastily, "there's such a long list of things that happened back then, I must have missed that one."

"It was during a pandemic," Patrick explained helpfully. "Someone was playing around with biotech under unsafe conditions, and... I guess they dropped a vial, or something. Then, during the panic, they did a total lockdown on the economy."

"Total?" Lisa frowned, straining to comprehend it. It didn't help that she was fairly unfamiliar with the incident in question. There had been so *much* that had gone on during the twentieth and twenty first centuries. There had even been multiple pandemics; she wasn't even certain which one Patrick was referring to. *Not the Spanish Flu?*

"Well, they shut down all the small businesses. And most of the entertainment industries," Patrick conceded.

Most? Surely a pandemic lockdown should have been absolute. Anything less than full quarantine wasn't going to do the trick. Of course, without properly automated infrastructure... "How did they avoid societal collapse?" she asked, glad of a distraction from her gnawing pit of a stomach, the way it had been twisting into knots over her repeated failures.

"They officially classified some of the workers as "essential," if they were working for the larger corporations," Patrick helpfully explained.

Lisa considered that. "For the same work that the smaller companies did?"

"Yep," came Patrick's laconic answer.

No wonder they called it the Dark Times, Lisa reflected. Every time she thought she had learned everything there was to know about the evils that went on back then, she learned something new. It wasn't just the larger issues, the genocides and the mounting tyrannies. It was also the seemingly minor details, the ingrained prejudices. The prevailing attitudes, the way people had been conditioned to casually accept the unacceptable. "And it was still during a pandemic," Lisa observed. "Didn't that expose them to the same disease?"

"Yep." Patrick shrugged again, his shoulders rising and falling. "A lot of them caught it. Repeatedly."

Lisa turned to stare out at the open water. The rippling of the waves was a soothing balm from the horrors of the topic of conversation. "Which pandemic was it? What disease?"

"Uh... Spanish Flu?" Now it was Patrick's turn to frown, as he struggled to recollect.

"No, Spanish Flu was the one where they were sending troops overseas and pretending the disease wasn't killing anyone," Lisa corrected him. "Where they had troop transports docking with holds full of corpses."

"You sure? I seem to recall the twenty first century was nonstop war. That "War of Terror" thing."

"War *on* Terror," Lisa corrected him, absently. Her gaze was focused on the water, the way the liquid churned with a deceptively mild appearance. The waves seemed gentle, slow, yet all that water carried vast amounts of power. What went on down there, where the native sapient life lived, so far from what humans could comfortably handle?

"That... that doesn't make sense," Patrick protested. "How do you make war *on* an emotion like terror?"

"Jingoistic rhetoric," Lisa replied dismissively. "A lot of meaningless propaganda to justify the endless feeding of the military-industrial complex."

"Oh. That thing," Patrick muttered. Possibly he was attempting to hide his ignorance of that particular bit of nastiness. *Doubtful. The M.I.C. was a major influence in the Dark Times.* The Fey would never have achieved a fraction of what they had, without species traitors who'd already proven themselves willing to slaughter their fellow human beings by the thousands, for short term personal gain.

Speaking of personal gain... "How well compensated are the fishermen, compared to the profits they were making before the fishing ban?" she asked.

Patrick paused to consider his answer. "For most of them, their total income's actually a bit higher than it is when they're working. They don't have the same expenses."

"But they're still upset about not being able to work..." Lisa mused. It made sense. Even when not pressured by survival constraints, humans still sought meaning in their existences. *Just look at me, for example*. She could have found a comfortable existence on some world or another, where her basic needs would be met. The sale of her ship and armor could have financed ample luxuries to guarantee a comfortable existence. And now, with the Fey hounding her, she could have easily corralled that into a paid early retirement, compensated by the Federation in exchange for the unpleasant situation that her services had placed her in.

No, she could never have given up her career. Her life on Gaia was a distant memory, she could never go back, but she was still a Gaian to the core. Every member of the tribe contributed, however and as much as they could. Lisa hunted. It was what she did. It was how she contributed. It was how she brought meaning to her own existence.

What would she have done, if someone prevented her from working her chosen profession, and bringing meaning to her life?

"So what are we doing now?" Patrick asked.

Lisa mentally kicked herself. She must have been silent for at least a minute there. But at least she had an answer for him. "I think we have some hard suspects now," she declared, attempting to sound more confident than she felt. "But I still need more information. I can't rule anything out just yet."

She felt like a pathetic fraud, making such a grandiose statement. But Patrick nodded in acknowledgment and did not call her out as such. Instead he offered a suggestion. "Want to get some lunch?"

Crap. Declining such an offer felt antisocial, humiliatingly so. She was doing her best to feign "eccentricity," but turning him down felt so... rude. "I'm sorry. I can't," she declined, the guilt writhing in her belly. *Or is that hunger?* "I need to do some more research in private."

Now Patrick evidenced amusement, one eyebrow arching as his lips quirked in a smile. Or possibly a smirk? "Did you want to get takeout, for when you're doing your research?"

Damn it. She could feel her cheeks flaming crimson; it was a good thing he couldn't see how fiercely she was blushing at his teasing. She bit her lip and inhaled deeply through her nose. *Deep breaths.* Then she exhaled heavily, before meekly replying, "...yes, please."

Chapter 18

Lisa wasn't even certain how to pronounce the name of the entree contained within the carton she had just opened. There was definitely an "-och" involved, though she couldn't remember where that particular syllable went. It was certainly a longish name, though, and it sounded as if someone had taken a few words of ethnic Mandarin, thrown in a bit of Gaelic, and then snickered at having just played a practical joke on any visiting tourists.

As for the dish itself, there was definitely a fair bit of egg involved. The main body of it seemed to be protein enriched rice, savory from the spice blend, but there were so many chopped vegetables mixed in that it gave the meal a multi-colored appearance. It was delicious and she could eat it with a spoon as she checked the computer terminal for something to look at, in the desperate hope that a clue would manifest itself in her inbox.

There didn't appear to be any clues, certainly not of the sort to make a Holmes jump upright and call out for Watson to make haste. There were a few ads, one for the newest scent of bath wash offered by her favorite purveyor of soaps; the other informing her of the latest selection of foodstuffs for stocking a ship's galley with. A bank statement for her primary account. A notice of the latest reviews of her professional services being linked to her website for potential customers to behold. And a few notifications from the Hunter's Guild.

Well, that ought to at least kill a little time. Lisa followed the link to the forum, to see what this was about – though she already suspected she knew what it was about. Sure enough, it was the thread she'd posted a comment on, while en route to Wigglebiggle. Someone had asked, either out of idle curiosity or genuine paranoia, how to handle a Fey encounter. And after everything Lisa had been through, she felt sufficiently qualified to chime in and share her opinion with others.

Changelings can't really do much more than subtly influence people, she had asserted. *It takes months, even years, for a changeling to have a serious effect. They use their powers in conjunction with more conventional methods of manipulation. Appealing to their victims' darker natures. Insecurities, fears, prejudices. It's no different from a human con artist, except the changeling con artist can tell what you're thinking.*

It was entirely factually correct, in her (admittedly limited) experience in dealing with the Fey. It certainly wasn't anything to drum up controversy, but... *Some people can't pass up an opportunity to be nasty.* In this case, people who posted on the Ultranet with a profile handle like Edgebane $X^{\wedge 3}$.

Edgebane $X^{\wedge 3}$ had quite the opinion of her post, and of herself. Lisa flinched under the condescending dismissal of herself, and of her advice, as the "pathetic attempts" of a "poseur tryhard." Yes, they were only words. Yes, she was too mature and well seasoned to care about such things. Yes, it still stung. Insults and nasty attacks always did. *Deep breaths.* She'd never even seen Edgebane $X^{\wedge 3}$ post a comment before;

surely she could dismiss an ignorant insinuation from a newbie who didn't know any better?

Bloodhound73's response to Edgebane X$^{\wedge 3}$'s comment was another matter. *LonehuntressGaia isn't a poseur. She's a serial killer.*

That hurt. And it wasn't even that she liked Bloodhound73, or even knew them beyond their bickerings on the Guild forum. Bloodhound73 was one of her most vitriolic detractors, and they simply would not stop. As far as they were concerned (whoever they were), Lisa was a bloodthirsty lunatic who used bounty hunting as an excuse to legally murder for pleasure.

Woah. Really? Edgebane X$^{\wedge 3}$ had asked.

Which had been a perfect opportunity for Bloodhound73 to launch into their usual tirade. *Her professional name is Lisa Huntress. Seriously. She calls herself Huntress, like it's her surname. She's a murderous lunatic who uses bounty hunting as an excuse to legally murder, for pleasure. The last time I checked, she was up to triple digits.*

The last time they'd checked? Even Lisa herself couldn't be certain of how many pirates she'd actually killed. It was difficult to do a head count when the heads weren't intact, and quite often they weren't. She didn't even keep a tally of kills, she kept a tally of jobs, of contracts. Bloodhound73 was just speculating, but they sounded so nastily... certain.

And the post went on! And on, and on, and on. A long description of some of the news stories about her, and about her own "trolling" at the Guild. Which was a rather biased way of describing her long-running series of arguments with a number of other forum members, including (but by no means limited to) Bloodhound73. It was all quite embarrassing, not to mention hurtful.

Why do they keep attacking me? They don't even know me!

But Edgebane X$^{\wedge 3}$ certainly seemed to be inclined to trust the word of Bloodhound73. *So has LoneHuntressGaia – excuse me, Lisa **Huntress** – ever actually dealt with the Fey?*

The next comment in the thread came from a name she found familiar, and the moment she read it she felt her heart catch in her throat. RagnarRedSkelton. She knew him. She had actually *met* him, owed him her life. It hadn't been a particularly friendly association, though. She had made a shamefully poor first impression – and the reason why was that she'd given him good reason to assume that all the stories about her bloodthirsty depravities were entirely true. Understated, even.

I know for a fact that she has, RagnarRedSkelton – or Red, as he liked to be called – had posted on the Ultranet. Judging by the timestamp, it had been while she'd been terrifying poor Director Stuart. *I took a search and rescue job that found her on a mining facility. From what I've gathered, the Fey are actively **hunting** Lisa.*

What. Seriously? Edgebane X$^{\wedge 3}$ was again prepared to trust the word of RagnarRedSkelton more readily than they had the word of LoneHuntressGaia.

Underneath this, Bloodhound73 had chimed in. *Was anyone else still alive when you got there? Or did she run out of victims before you arrived?*

Ouch. Ow, that hurt. It wouldn't hurt so much if it weren't so true. *I turned that place into a slaughterhouse.* She had been so angry, so furious at the damage to her vessel (and her personal possessions, left exposed to the blending of her ship's oxygen supply with an alien atmosphere rich in hydrogen sulfide). She'd had to commandeer a craft not meant for someone her size, stuck in cramped confinement for more than six hours before arriving at that facility. At which point she had taken out her frustrations upon the idiots who had failed in their attempts to murder her.

The sounds of their panicked screams over the intercepted communications had been most enjoyable to listen to, at the time. Not so much afterwards, when she'd found herself sleeping in their beds, looking at their personal possessions. Being forcibly reminded that, whatever else they had been, they were still thinking, feeling individuals, with lives and histories. The memory of a middle aged woman's face, wreathed in both terror, desperate hope, and something *else* that Lisa had never quite been able to puzzle out came to her. And a coffee mug, held up in an invitation that had met with lethal rejection.

But RagnarRedSkelton was rising to her defense, and it was both shocking and gratifying to read his words. *Apparently they were actively trying to kill her. I honestly don't think she would have killed anyone if they hadn't been trying so hard. I had to ferry her ship back to a spaceport, and I saw the damage. Whatever went on back there, it was definitely a mutual hostility.*

Lisa felt a rush of validation at his words. It felt... good, to have someone defend her like that. To stand up to Bloodhound73 and the others, and dispute their (mostly) unfounded accusations.

But Edgebane $X^{\wedge 3}$ did indeed have more questions, though they were at least prepared to trust RagnarRedSkelton's words over those of Bloodhound73. *So what was her original name?*

By this point Lisa had finished the delicious rice dish, and was now moving on to the *bao*, the steamed buns with their richly spiced meat filling. They were definitely near the top of her personal list of Wigglebiggle's culinary delights, and she'd grabbed a dozen, six to each bag, to accompany her meal. And someone named Sunset○62869 had chimed in to respond to that question. *I don't know where you're from, but it's considered rude in most cultures to ask about abandoned names. Show respect for others, by addressing them by their preferred name.*

Lisa couldn't help but notice the use of a spice she'd never tasted before. There was heat to it, yes, but there was also a faint citrus taste to it. She also noticed that she had reached the end of the thread. There had been no new comments since Sunset062869's reprimand.

Well, why not? She felt a bit emboldened by the unexpected support from Red, bold enough to answer Edgebane $X^{\wedge 3}$'s question. Taking another bite of *bao*, she leaned forward and inputted a response. *My own cultural traditions dictate the use of the profession as a surname. As a child I was simply "Lisa." I always looked forward to calling myself Lisa Huntress when I grew up.* After pausing to consider what else to say, she popped the rest of the bun into her mouth and continued. *And yes, the hostility was very much mutual. The people aboard that facility had originally been involved in some illicit mining operation. For what it's worth, I don't think any of them ever suspected that their supervisor was a changeling. But they did try to kill me. It was not a pleasant experience.*

On the other hand, eating the buns was very much a pleasant experience. A carafe of green tea provided ample liquid for washing it all down, and by the time she was down to a final bun waiting forlornly at the bottom of the bag, there was another notification. Edgebane $X^{\wedge 3}$ was asking if she could share more information about dealing with the Fey. They were asking... politely. It was most gratifying.

Changelings have very subtle powers, she elaborated. *They can make you think they look different than they really do, but otherwise they mostly just manipulate like any other con artist. I can't say much about the abilities of full blooded Fey. I've only ever encountered one*

"Fey Lord," but I can say that it was able to project thoughts, not just read them.

Unlike the squeezebulbs she kept aboard the *Hearth*, the Gonganting's supply of tableware tended towards more traditional cups and mugs. Her mug could contain a half a pint of liquid, which was a decent amount for a normal person. Not so much for a woman of her mass, who had just consumed six *bao* after her main course. She poured herself another cup to help wash it all down. As she stirred the sweetener into the tea, she saw another notification. Edgebane $X^{\wedge 3}$ wished to know what sort of thoughts the Fey Lord had projected at her.

Lisa flinched. *I brought this on myself.* It was painful to remember – she was still trying to recover from the experience. But she had offered to share the knowledge and they were asking for her to act on that offer; she couldn't very well stop now. Lisa bit her lip and braced herself to share her personal trauma with interested strangers.

Waves of negative thoughts, she explained. Then she mentally chided herself. That wasn't nearly detailed enough to describe what that eldritch abomination had done. *It made me believe I was weak,* she went on, remembering how *true* it had all seemed to her, when those thoughts had been pushed into her head as if they were her own. *Stupid. Pathetic. Incompetent. Helpless. It made me think those things as if they were my own thoughts. To make me believe I had already lost, so I wouldn't even try to fight back.*

Lisa closed her eyes and shuddered, taking a deep breath. She hadn't lost. She had won. It was important to remember that. And it was important to explain why, and how. After all, that was the reason for the Fey's continual harassment. They didn't want other humans to learn how to resist their influence. Ergo...

It brushed against some personal psychological trauma, from my past. She was very careful to avoid specificity about the nature of that trauma. She didn't want anyone on the forum to know just what had happened to her. What had been done to her. Who had done it to her. *I don't think it was expecting me to respond with anger. I was able to damage it, and that greatly lessened the assault.*

Lisa sent the comment firing off into the interstellar communications grid that was the Ultranet, then reached for her tea to sip as she tried to center herself. A steady swallow, then a deep inhalation. Then an exhalation, before sipping again and repeating the process. *Deep breaths.* Though strangely enough, she felt rather less upset about sharing the painful recollections than she had expected to.

Another response came from Edgebane $X^{\wedge 3}$. *How did you damage it?*

Lisa set her mug down and answered the question. *I cut off one of its legs, and its telepathic assault became... staticky. As if there were some kind of interference. But it was still broadcasting, until I crushed its head.* She posted the answer, then went back to sipping at her tea.

She had almost finished the mug by the time Edgebane $X^{\wedge 3}$ posted another comment. *Maybe it's not just the one Fey that was doing it? What if it's their entire species behind the assaults? They're a hive mind, right? So, maybe the Fey Lord was just a conduit? That would mean the static was because the conduit was damaged. That would also explain why changelings aren't as powerful. They're less effective as conduits, on account of being partly human.*

Lisa blinked, then stared at the screen with widening eyes. That... made a great deal of sense. *You might be right,* she replied, feeling genuinely impressed with Edgebane $X^{\wedge 3}$'s insight. *If anyone has more questions, I'll do my best to answer. If someone like me can resist the Fey, anyone can.*

She leaned back in her chair (ignoring the way it creaked ever so slightly from the strain), holding the mostly empty mug with both hands. After all the frustrations from her fruitless investigation, basking in the respectful admiration of another felt like a tonic for the soul.

Besides, the Overone keeps trying to hurt me. It feels good to return the favor.

Chapter 19

It was very, very late. Or possibly very, very early, depending on one's view. Lisa's own view was that it was very, very late – far later than she would have liked. But she had been desperate for a clue, for a development, something to help her achieve her Holmes-ian denouement. The entire colony was depending on it, on her.

Thankfully, regardless of whatever grievances or motives Chief Callan might have for her barely concealed fixation, she was at least agreeable to polite requests. Lisa had forced herself to address the Chief Jingcha as "Chun," as if they were on friendly terms, as if the woman hadn't been making barely-concealed investigative movements around her. Lisa knew – she *knew* – that Chun Callan had been investigating her. There had been a few slips of the tongue, about foods she enjoyed. About her professional record. Lisa was a hunter, first and foremost, and she knew she was being hunted. *I just wish I knew why*.

But if Callan was hunting her, she was at least allowing Lisa to run to ground, to handle the investigation before springing whatever trap the Chief Jingcha had been planning.

A politely coached request had resulted in Chief Callan fetching a set of keys from the governor. Keys to a warehouse containing some valuable government property. Specifically, almost a hundred surveillance drones, officially purposed for geological surveys. Not that anyone appeared to be inclined to object to their serving double duty as part of a murder investigation.

Lisa was no expert, but she didn't have to be. The colony's drones were cheap, simple, and idiot-resistant(the expression "idiot-proof" having long since been discontinued, courtesy of stringent regulations regarding false advertising). They largely consisted of an anti-gravity generator, a sensor suite, and little else. It had been a simple matter to program nine of them to move about in extremely basic patterns, back and forth over the coastline. The tenth monitored the docks, purely as a formality. Nobody would be stupid enough to take a boat straight from the docks.

That had been hours ago. So much of hunting was about patience. Particularly when it came to laying in wait for the quarry to show up. Lisa had sat down with a kilo of boneless fried chicken strips, a liter of roasted and salted soybeans, three liter bottles of green tea at room temperature, and with an audio book about Sharon Holmes and the Case of the Siamese Fighting Fish. She was now down to a few paltry strips of chicken, an empty greasy container smelling of salt and soy, a half a bottle of green tea, and Professor Watson's anguished realization that the colleague he so idolized was well aware of his mounting attraction to her.

By this point Lisa's brain had become so saturated with Sherlock Holmes mythology that she had begun to critique the different versions. *This sucks.* The romantic subplot was detracting from the main plot of the mystery, she felt. *I want to know why the fish food flakes were so important.*

The audio book abruptly stopped playing, truncating Sharon's intrigued speculations into nothing more than the opening observations of Watson's quickened breath and elevated heart rate. For just a moment, Lisa felt a brief twinge of annoyance at not getting to find out if Sharon would call attention to the most obvious sign of masculine arousal. But the audio book had automatically stopped because the motion sensors on one of the drones had registered at least one human sized object.

Two, in fact. They were skulking about, and in the stupidest possible place. *No. This is a false alarm. Those must be dock workers. Or they're just checking on their boat.* There was a total ban on fishing and sailing, until easement rights had been negotiated with the Octopussies. Even going out onto the water was considered a violation of their territory at present. But boats being kept in dock probably still needed maintenance, and most likely had a few things kept in storage to be retrieved.

No, they really are sneaking out from the docks. Lisa now had confirmation. They truly were, beyond any reasonable doubt, a pair of absolute idiots. They were barely even trying to hide it, as they untied the ropes and began to disembark.

For a moment, she considered informing Chief Jingcha Callan. But it was still dark out, the woman was almost certainly asleep, and Lisa did not want to antagonize her any more than necessary. In the meantime she could have the drone follow them, recording their criminal behavior.

And what behavior it was. *Poaching. Got you, you bastards.* She could only hope they were the same pair that had humiliated her so thoroughly the previous day. It would be oh so satisfying to haul them in like the nets they were preparing to cast into the water.

Then she saw the tentacles rising out of the water.

Crap!

She could only watch the monitor in mute horror as the suckered tendrils lashed out at the boat — and at the two poachers. As the first man was yanked overboard and sent headfirst into the roiling ocean water, Lisa realized she was watching an interspecies incident in progress.

Did those two idiots just start a war!?

Chapter 20

Archie was glad to have company. It was a lonely feeling, violating an unjust law by yourself. Even one accomplice was sufficient to make a revolutionary feel as if he weren't fighting the entire world by himself. Because their government had betrayed them, and so had the Federation, and it was time to take a stand on behalf of the people of Varuna.

Besides, it took at least two men to work the nets. Archie could sail the *Yíchǎn* by himself, but he'd need a hand if he was going to haul in the fish.

I am so done with this pile of tǔ.

They had made a home for themselves. This was their *home*. This was the only home Archie had ever known. Not just the planet, but this boat, his grandfather's boat. He still remembered the first time he'd climbed aboard, barely older than a toddler as his father introduced him to the *Yíchǎn* and called her a member of the family. Big sis *Yíchǎn*.

Archie's boots made soft clopping noises as he made his way toward's the sampan's rudder. His grandfather, Angus, had built it by slicing a storage container in half, making a half cylinder out of the tough, durable, waterproof and weather resistant polymer. Archie took hold of the tiller, clicking the switch to activate the water pump. Below the surface of the water, the pump attached to the rudder began to suck in water and spit it out, in a continuous and silent stream. Smoothly and quietly, the sampan sailed away from the dock.

Finfan had settled on one of the crossboards that bridged the width of the *Yíchǎn*. Archie had resurfaced them with fresh padding a few years before his father had decided to retire, so the old man would have something more comfortable to sit on, whilst on the way to cast the nets. It would be another decade or so before the material began to flake and crack like the old seating had, and it was nice to have something comfortable to rest one's arse upon, when one's job involved sitting for long periods. Archie could feel the padding against his own buttocks, and it was such a welcome feeling indeed.

This is what the squid things took from me.

They wanted to claim that *he* wasn't a native? This was *his* world. He'd earned the right to live here. His parents, his grandparents, they had helped build their home with hard work and sweat. It hadn't been free of risk or sacrifice, either. Or of tragedy. Archie had only known *one* grandfather, and only *one* grandmother. His mother's father had died constructing the underwater turbines for one of the hydroelectric plants, crushed underwater when a line had snapped. And his own father, Alec Wang, had lost his mother when he was still young, during the malnutrition epidemic (before the Federation had provided emergency shipments of food and phosphorous, until their own crops could provide the necessary nutrition).

The stars were visible, but otherwise it was so dark as to

be almost pitch black. Yet Archie was headed towards his favorite spot to cast nets for sardines, with unerring accuracy as he navigated through the darkness of the early morning. He knew exactly where he was going, needing only the stars in the sky to guide his way. They were *his* stars. This was *his* night sky. He knew the constellations by heart. The Duck. The Flag. The Squabbling Couple. Constellations named over three generations, to guide sailors charting their way across the Varuna oceans. Archie knew them as well as he knew the currents, and the migration patterns of the fish. Right now there were sardines swimming about in the cool waters near the surface, nibbling at the plankton drifting on the currents while enjoying the relative safety of darkness. Once the sun rose they would swim deeper, avoiding the warmer waters and diving down to take refuge amongst the seabed flora. Which made early morning the best time for catching them.

Finfan belched and reached out one hand, lazily drifting his fingers through the water. "About there," he observed mildly, with the calm assurance of an old seadog. Finfan had been working on fishing boats for even longer than Archie had; he'd been a young deckhand when Archie's father Alec had still been running the *Yichǎn*. Once old Alec had decided to spend his declining years playing with his grandchildren, Finfan had worked for his old school chum Archie. And for their other former classmates, any captain needing a hand with the nets.

This was the life! This was *Archie's* life! This was everything he'd ever wanted. He had been *content* with this. He hadn't wanted much. Just to be sailing his beloved big sis *Yichǎn* out to sea, before morning during the summer months when the sardines were teeming. The larger, more predatory fish during the Varuna autumn, when everything was breeding and feasting and preparing to die. The prawns and lobsters during the winter.

He was sick of hanging around the pub. So was Finfan. They'd both had enough of bending over backwards at the whims of those disgusting tentacled pranksters, and the dictates of Federation file sorters who'd never even set foot on Varuna. Archie was so very *done* with it all. It was time to get back to what he knew best. And what Finfan knew best; the man was already popping open the crates containing the nets. It was time to cast and catch a haul, to fill the bellies of good people who deserved more than just vat cloned meats.

Their callused hands seized up the carefully rolled netting with practiced ease, as they lifted and separated. Strong arms hoisted the braided strands upwards, ready to throw. Once the ends were tossed the nets would unfurl automatically, sinking slightly into the water. Then they'd just have to engage the water pumps and move forward, and scoop up a nice big haul.

Archie certainly wasn't expecting to be scooped up first.

Both fishermen were too shocked and confused by the initial eruption to recognize the long, sinuous objects almost exploding out of the water. Several of them slammed down on the gunwale, coiling about over the rim. Archie couldn't make out any details, it was still too dark to see anything clearly. Then two more of the long, dripping wet tendrils slapped against Archie's arms, knocking them into his own torso. He was being restrained! He was being wrapped up by those... *tentacles.*

The bastards got us.

Archie heard the splash as Finfan was pulled into the water, and felt his boots leaving the deck. His own body was being spun through the air as the octopussy yanked him upwards, pulling him in a circular arc towards the ocean.

"Fuuuu..." he began to scream, before cold seawater slammed into his face and open mouth.

He squirmed and struggled, desperate to at least get his head above the surface. He could only be grateful for having the presence of mind to close his throat off with his tongue, to spit out the seawater before he swallowed any. Varuna's ocean water was decidedly toxic to humans if ingested, much like the seawater of Earth.

My knife. Like any sailor with an ounce of sense, Archie carried a knife with him at all times. His own favored blade was still safely stowed in its sheath against his hip. The forward curving hook shape was perfect for tearing into things like a razor edged talon, and the edge could slice through even the tough cords of the netting with just a little bit of sawing. It would be perfect for hacking through these tentacles... *but I can't reach it.* His arms were pressed to his sides by the tentacles wrapped around him, and his fingers were only able to brush the bottom of the sheath. He couldn't manage to get them up towards the handle and restraining strap.

Archie gasped for breath as his head finally breached the surface, and he blinked and glared about wildly. He couldn't see! Everything was dark! His legs were kicking as he tried to tread water, but he was beginning to realize *that* wasn't what was keeping him afloat. The tentacles were holding him fast, and the monster was clinging to the side of the *Yíchǎn*.

Get off my damned boat! Archie wanted to scream at the disgusting monster. But he was busy coughing and trying not to inhale seawater as the monster's thrashings churned up the surface of the water. He was helpless in its grasp, forcibly reminded of what every sailor learned and relearned, again and again. The sea was vast, mysterious, and dangerous, and their boats literally skimmed the mere surface of something far greater, far more terrible, than anything they could hope to master.

Then Archie beheld a huge eye glaring at him, from mere centimeters away. Its terrible beak was on the underside of the head, surrounded by the base of the tentacles. The tentacles that brought captured prey to that beak...

Archie closed his eyes and clenched his teeth, shutting out that terrible eye. He knew what was coming, and he could only pray for it to be over quickly.

Chapter 21

Lisa's deliberately cultivated *eccentricity* was proving to be surprisingly utilitarian, at times like this. Lisa in comfortable clothing was an explosively athletic powerhouse. Lisa in powered armor was a bipedal mobile weapon capable of traversing a kilometer of flat terrain in under a minute, or even faster if she employed her thruster jets for the added boost. It was a very useful feature.

It would have been even more useful if the docks weren't already within walking distance of the Gonganting. Lisa's explosive rush to the docks only gave her a minute of headstart on Chief Jingcha Callan, who had trotted out after the bounty hunter with a sleep deprived groan and a shirt still being tugged over her midsection. The two of them came to a halt at the beginning of the docks, standing side by side as they glared out at the starlit ocean. The foremost law enforcement authority on the planet, radiating an enraged aura of frustration and resolve, shoulder to shoulder with the armor clad bounty hunter.

After a few moments, it occurred to Lisa to raise a point of inquiry. "So what are we supposed to do now?"

"There's nothing we can do," Chun sighed, still staring out at the horizon. "We just wait."

They waited. At least the sky was beginning to lighten, as the dawn began to approach. The stars were beginning to fade, as the steadily increasing light washed them away from the naked eye. Black became a dark, deep purple, and then a lighter, grayish shade of violet. Until the far sky began to take on reddish hues. Then the gold appeared, like a blood tipped disc of antiquated splendor from some ancient treasure trove. The green was a nice touch; not every sky managed to achieve shades of green before the sun's rim began to appear over the horizon.

As Wigglebiggle's sun began to climb more fully into view, Lisa felt obliged to comment. "That's beautiful." She meant it. She had watched the sun rise on multiple planets, but a sunrise was always a beautiful sight to behold, regardless of the world, regardless of the sun.

"Yes," Callan agreed, her eyes darting to the side as she glanced at the armored figure. "I was hoping to share a sunrise with you, while you were here."

What the hell does that mean? Lisa knew that Callan was investigating her, for some strange reason. Her working theory at this point was that Callan was a lurker on the Hunter's Guild, convinced by the likes of Bloodhound73 that she was a menace to the society that the Jingcha were sworn to protect. That would certainly be more than sufficient motivation to keep a wary eye upon Lisa, if Callan was convinced she was a, a... *a legalized serial killer.*

But something was catching her attention, and her left hand shot out to point at the horizon. "There! They're coming!"

"You can see them?" Callan asked, sounding surprised. She

peered out over the horizon, squinting with the effort of attempting to locate the dot in the distance.

Crap, Lisa belatedly realized. "My helmet has a zoom feature built in," she explained. She almost added – but did not, catching herself before she revealed a potential vulnerability – an explanation about being naturally nearsighted, courtesy of her Gaian heritage.

"Oh, right," Callan agreed. "I forgot about that. Our construction suits have some visual enhancement features." She sighed, adding in a rueful tone, "Not that I've ever used one. At least, not outside basic Jingcha training."

"Oh?" Lisa found herself warming to the conversation despite herself, now that they were discussing a topic familiar to her. "You've never needed to put one on, to track down a criminal?"

"It's never come up," Callan shrugged. "I've been in my share of brawls, but I was either in my uniform, or in my civvies. Except for that time I... uh..." She trailed off suddenly, turning her head away to look in a different direction.

"Except for what time?" Lisa asked, her curiosity piqued.

Callan gulped, then coughed to clear her throat. "Ahem. Except for the time... well... ahem." She cleared her throat again, before confessing. "It was... well, it was at a massage parlor. I was... well, I was being worked on..."

Lisa turned to peer down at the woman. Behind her helmet's protective cover, Lisa's eyes widened slightly. *Is she... blushing?* "So what happened?"

"Um..." Callan made a soft little grunt, then forced out an answer. "A domestic dispute broke out. It got violent, and I had to rush out and deal with it."

"Oh." Lisa considered that for a moment, then realized

she was missing an important piece of information. "So what were you wearing, while you were being "worked on?""

Callan sighed. "A towel." Then, in a slightly strangled tone, she added, "it slipped. During the... altercation."

Lisa said nothing for a period of time, as she digested this information. Finally, she thought of something to say in response. "But you dealt with the situation, right?"

"Yes," Callan confirmed. "In fact, it was over before I even realized the towel had fallen off. I had both of them on the ground, and then I... well, I had to keep holding them until someone on duty could take them off my hands..."

Small wonder the woman felt embarrassed. She would have had to give everyone present, including her colleagues, a full show, lest she be delinquent in her responsibilities, or allow potentially dangerous individuals out of whatever hold she had them in. *That must have been so humiliating!*

A sense of growing camaraderie led Lisa to admit, "I did something like that, once. I was transporting a prisoner, and he was... dangerous. I had to buy a metal cage and keep him in it, just to keep him secure."

"Why didn't you just put him in your... oh, you don't have a brig," Callan answered her own question. "But don't you have an auto-doc? You could have shoved him there, and kept him sedated."

"I suppose. This seemed more secure," Lisa shrugged, though her armor largely concealed the movement of her shoulders and upper torso. "Electronic mechanisms can be bypassed. Metal bars and chains are a lot harder to get past."

"Chains and cages?" Callan murmured. "Hmm..."

Lisa blushed beet red beneath her helmet. "*Anyway,* when I thought he was making another escape attempt, I jumped out of bed and went to check."

"Oh, so he caught you in your nightgown?" Callan asked,

and there was the strangest expression on her face. "Or were you..."

"Not even a towel," Lisa admitted.

The Chief Jingcha stared at her for a long moment, then burst into giggles. After a moment the deep, resonant boom of Lisa's own laughter, amplified by her helmet's audio output, rang out over the ocean waves. It was the first time Lisa had actually laughed about the incident. For that matter, it was the first time she'd told anyone about the incident. It felt... good, to share a laugh about it.

Wait. Was this an attempt by Callan to get Lisa to lower her guard? A well trained law enforcement officer was versed in interrogation techniques, after all. *Real interrogation techniques. Not the ham-fisted stuff you've tried.* The memory of *that* particular shame hit with sudden clarity, dampening her good humor. Lisa sobered and watched the approaching boat.

It was being piloted by... *an Octopussy?*

The alien creature had clearly figured out how to operate the craft. One tentacle was wrapped around the tiller, and it appeared to be enjoying itself tremendously. Two more tentacles gripped at the crossboard it perched upon, as a human pilot might. Its remaining tentacles were furled up in two thick balls, like clenched fists. It was fairly obvious what the Octopussy was holding.

Are they still alive?

Behind Lisa, additional Jingchas were approaching, as were several individuals clad in white uniforms that clearly identified them as medical personnel. They all awaited the arrival of the boat, and instructions from Callan.

Finally the boat came up alongside the pier, in a clumsy but relatively well executed docking attempt. The Octopussy released its hold upon the crossboard and slithered onto the dock, tossing the two bodies down at the bemused Chief's feet. Then the artificially generated voice, thankfully set to its usual high pitched range, rang out from the Octopussy's translator.

"You're **nicked**, chums! Book em, Chief!"

Callan glanced down at the two coughing, gasping, trembling men at her feet. Then she glanced at Lisa. Then she turned back to her invertebrate subordinate, before sighing heavily. "Just... fine. Medics? Check them both out, take care of them. Spatchcock, Morely, get that boat moored – *carefully*, don't damage it. Tako..." Callan shook her head, closing her eyes as her face scrunched up in frustration, before relaxing into weary resignation. "You... you did good."

Jingcha Tako quivered at his Chief's praise. "Does this mean a promotion?"

"It means you can have your badge back," Callan growled.

As the two continued to bicker, Lisa looked down at the two fishermen. *I know these two.* They were coughing and crying as the medics took their vitals and wrapped them in water absorbing blankets to dry and warm them, but they were unmistakably the two fishermen that Lisa had completely and utterly failed to impress at the pub the previous day.

As she stared down at them, a sudden epiphany came to her.

I need to go to bed. Lisa had been up all night, she was entirely superfluous to the current situation, and even if she weren't, she was far, far too tired to deal with it. She turned away and trudged off, leaving the Chief Jingchua to handle things, while Lisa sought recuperative slumber.

Chapter 22

Lisa didn't want to get up. Her mouth was dry, her bladder was full, and yet she was still so tired. Her legs in particular were suggesting that she simply relax, and let the cleaning service deal with the aftermath.

It was that last thought that compelled her to roll out of the bed. Lisa had no wish to inflict such unpleasantness upon others, whether it was a human doing the cleaning or even just a drone. *And in a colony like this one, it'll probably be a human.* Wigglebiggle lacked the technological abundance of older, more settled worlds. No, she would simply have to force herself to shamble off in search of the toilet.

By the time she had finished emptying her bladder, and washing out her mouth with a cool drink of tap water, Lisa felt sufficiently awake for a more comprehensive status check. First, the time. Late afternoon, apparently. Next, the food supply. Decidedly depleted, both chicken strips and soybeans now a distant memory. Her armor's energy reserves were fully topped off, she'd be able to go on a food run before attempting to deal with the investigation.

The investigation...

Thus far the "eccentric" Huntress had achieved absolutely nothing of any redeeming value. It was almost a week since her arrival, and what had she managed to accomplish? *I binge watched old shows, played some video games, and stuffed my face.* She couldn't even claim credit for catching the poachers; Tako had been the one to apprehend them. At the very most she could say that she'd provided evidence to confirm their guilt. *Playing a supporting role to an alien cop who thinks it's a game. They're not getting their money's worth.*

Lisa almost bumped into the Governor on her way to Callan's office. Fortunately for both him, and the box he was carrying, she managed to avoid impacting him with her armored bulk. "I'm sorry!" she reflexively blurted out, before mentally kicking herself for sounding like a naughty child.

"It's okay," he said, lifting up the box as if using it to shield himself from the armored bounty hunter. "I was just bringing Chun some shortbread."

"Oh." Lisa gave the box a closer inspection, curious as to the contents. And the source, so that she could go grab a box for herself. Shortbread sounded pretty good at the moment.

"Did you... want some?" Patrick asked, looking up at her helmet with an inquisitive expression.

Crap. Politely declining the invitations was becoming increasingly difficult. Particularly the "politely" aspect of it; she was uncomfortably aware that she was coming across as antisocial. She attempted to divert the line of questioning by suggesting, "I don't know if Chief Callan would want to share her shortbread with me."

The Governor's mouth quirked slightly. "She'd like to share a lot more than shortbread with you," he dryly observed.

So. He knew. Could he confirm her working theory about Callan being prejudiced against her by Ultranet rumors, or if there was some other reason for the woman's obsessively suspicious demeanor? "So why does she want to put me in shackles, anyway?" Lisa asked, doing her best to keep her tones as casual and nonchalant as possible.

Patrick did a double take, his eyes widening at Lisa's words. His cheeks... *flushed? Is he blushing?* His mouth worked silently for a few seconds before he coughed delicately. "Ahem... I didn't realize she was that... kinky..." he murmured, glancing away in embarrassment.

What is he talking about? A sudden worry came to mind; surely Wigglebiggle observed standard Federation guidelines for minimum requirements in regards to judicial punishments and professionalism? Surely they weren't so barbaric as to include... *that*... as punitive retribution for criminal transgressions? That was straight out of the Dark Times! Or earlier, even; judicial rape was absolutely archaic in its barbarity.

Then another – considerably more humiliating – suspicion came to mind. "Are we... are we talking about two different things, here?" she asked tentatively, even as the horrible certainty settled upon her.

"That depends," the Governor replied slowly, still clutching the container of shortbread in both hands. "What are *you* talking about?"

Behind the concealment of her helmet, Lisa closed her eyes and felt the flush spread over her face. *Now he knows what a screwup I am.* "She wants to... arrest me, for something. I don't know why. She's been... investigating me..." Lisa trailed off into silence as she withered under Patrick's incredulous stare.

Great. Now he knows he hired an incompetent. Lisa would have already fled in search of a place to cry in solitude, but simple courtesy kept her in place. This man deserved the chance to yell at her first. She kept her eyes shut and waited for the outburst.

Finally it came, in a soft, almost disbelieving tone. As if the Governor truly could not believe the sheer depths of Lisa's staggering incompetence.

"Chun investigated you before you ever showed up," he murmured. "She couldn't stop gushing about you."

Lisa opened her eyes and stared down at the man. Once again she couldn't help but note, in the tiny part of her mind that was observing the rest of the ongoing disaster for future recollection, how people kept tilting their heads to look *up* at her, even though she felt like a child under their withering stares. "Gushing?"

"Oh, yeah," Patrick affirmed, nodding his head vigorously. "She *wants* you. If shackles get involved, that's between the two of you. I've got my Moira; Chun can have you."

Have me? Lisa's blush had spread to the back of her neck, a hot, deeply uncomfortable sensation. "She doesn't even know what I look like," the Huntress protested weakly.

"No..." Patrick replied slowly, his expression shifting slightly. "There's pictures in the official records."

Crap. Of course there were pictures. Lisa lived in a technologically advanced society, and Wigglebiggle had had three generations to set up at least a handful of satellites for Ultranet access. Even if they lacked a proper localized internet of their own – and that was a big *if* – they would still have access to the rest of the Federation. *At least the pictures would mostly be just of my face.*

"Plus, I think she's found some videos and images taken from a planet called New Athens," Patrick provided helpfully. "The catsuit looked good on you. Er, don't tell Moira I said that," he hastily added.

Oh, gods. Lisa closed her eyes again, silently replaying every interaction she'd had with Chief Jingchua Chun Callan in her mind. Seen through a different lens, the woman's behavior took on a decidedly... different tonality. *New Athens. Sara.* The memory of Lisa's first consensual sex partner, her first love, hit her already befuddled brain with a jarringly painful impact. It had been considerably less than a year since she'd found, then lost Sara. Even the joys of her relationships with Harvey, Brutus, and Jenny did little to soften the pain.

Then came the thought of Chief Callan in a classic New Athenian outfit, such as the school uniform-inspired attire that Sara had favored. Hanging on Lisa's arm as they walked in a park. *Is **that** what she's been hoping to achieve? Is **that** why she's been hunting me?*

Lisa didn't even know *how* to feel about it. She couldn't decide whether to be flattered by the attention, or offended at the invasion of privacy, or nervous at having a powerful and well connected client crushing on her. She settled for her default reaction of terrified humiliation at being the center of anyone's attention.

"So... you really didn't know?" Patrick asked, sounding genuinely surprised. Lisa opened her eyes again to see him staring up at her helmeted visage.

"I'm... not used to people finding me attractive..." Lisa confessed.

"Small wonder. You keep hiding away in that armor," the Governor pointed out. "How can you get used to it, if you keep hiding in your armor?"

Patrick flinched slightly, taking a cautious step backwards. Lisa couldn't blame him; she had just winced so hard at his words that it had been visible even through her massive, heavily protective suit. His words had just hit home with painful accuracy. *But I'm scared of people!* Lisa wanted to protest. Which was... not the sort of thing that he needed to be hearing from the FIA operative he was depending upon for the future of his world. "You... you do have a point..."

"Huh." Patrick shook his head and looked quietly contemplative. "You really didn't know. I guess it's true what they say."

What's true? "What do they say?" Lisa asked.

"Oh." Patrick shrugged diffidently. "It's easy to see it from the outside. Not so much when you're involved in it." He sniffed delicately before adding, "still, I thought seeing other people's points of view was one of the skills you investigators pick up."

Ouch. That hurt, and not just because he had just received yet another clue as to her fraudulent nature. Empathy, understanding the thought processes and behavioral patterns of others, was a valuable skill for a hunter. You literally *couldn't* hunt a Gaian monkey spider without it. The nightmarish ambush predators of the forest's understory relied on launching themselves at prey like a slingshot, using their long, thin limbs to propel themselves faster than a human could move.

But if you knew where they were, and what they were intending, you could brace your spear and deliberately trigger their assault – and the monkey spider would impale itself like skewered meat.

Lisa had even managed to replicate John Tribe's method of using bait to deal with gruzzles, in order to turn the tables on her would-be assassins not too long ago. Lisa *knew* how to use her empathy to hunt, dammit! She should have realized. She *knew* how to empathize, how to see through the eyes of others...

The eyes of others.

Holy crap. Could that be it? Was it really that simple?

"I think I just found a lead," she breathed, eyes widening behind her helmet at the sudden epiphany.

Patrick looked decidedly impressed at the tone of awed elation in her voice. "You think so? Are you... about to crack the case?"

"I... I think I might be," Lisa agreed. She looked down at him, at the shortbread, and mentally kicked herself yet again. *So many wasted opportunities. So much **food** I didn't get to eat!* All because she'd been stupid enough to think "being eccentric" would help. When what she'd really needed to do was to force herself out of her own comfort zone and start *talking* to people.

Including the invertebrate people.

Callan glanced up in surprise as Lisa burst into her office. "Is Jingchua Tako available to talk?" the Huntress blurted out by way of greeting.

The Chief stared at Lisa, before her eyes glanced to just behind the armored hulk. Patrick was ambling in with a bemused but laconic expression. Then Callan glanced back at Lisa and she replied, "He's off duty right now, so he's probably hanging out with his friends."

Crap. If he'd tossed his badge and slithered back into the ocean again, Lisa would just have to wait for him to return. She felt her elation fading.

"His human friends," Chun added.

Lisa's elation surged again. *Perfect.* She needed answers, and Tako was her best bet for helping her understand the most important mindset of all for this case.

Ambassador Sashimi.

Chapter 23

Of course Tako was in his holding tank, being an aquatic life form. For Wigglebiggle's first Octopussy Jingcha, spending time with friends involved folding chairs and a massive display screen kept securely attached to a stand some distance away. Lisa approached just in time to see an anthromorphic wolf being crushed flat beneath a falling boulder, as a rabbit leered down from the top of a cliff. Literally, crushed *flat*, the boulder rolling away to reveal a lupine pancake. A two-dimensional arm raised up, brandishing a spatula as the wolf attempted to extricate his deformed body.

Lisa couldn't help but chuckle. Slapstick cartoons had been a staple entertainment for a thousand years, predating even the development of animation techniques. Art depicting comical levels of violence and exaggerated features had already existed long before someone figured out how to fool the human eye by flashing a succession of gradually modified images to create the illusion of movement. Then the rise of digital tools to assist in creation had made the production of stylized animated artwork a cost effective form of recreation for generation after generation, ever since. Even people working in asteroid mining facilities with minimal resources, or living in quonset huts while the hostile atmosphere of their newly colonized planet were being terraformed, could enjoy two-dimensional characters pounding each other like elastic stress-relieving toys. Also shooting each other, slicing and stabbing, immolating and cooking, blowing up, electrocuting, and whatever sort of darkly comedic pain the artists could conceive.

A memory came to her, then. An electronic tablet held in chubby little digits, as she sat on baked clay and followed along. *Peter Prey*. She hadn't thought about Peter Prey in so very long. Peter Prey and Tommy Tourist. The children of the tribe had learned math and science on the tablets as they'd grown older, but their first lessons were from Peter Prey, who was always keeping ahead of the Thuggees, using his brains to foil the schemes of the cartoonish caricatures of very real monsters that had always been seen as the greatest threat the Gaians faced, in their daily lives. And Tommy Tourist, the endlessly respawning offworlder who mocked Peter as a spear chucking primitive, only to end up being killed at the hands of Thuggees. And Gruzzles. And Monkey Spiders. And trapper plants, falls from trees, voracious insects, spoiled water and food, improperly tended fires, improperly maintained equipment, and even (in one particularly memorable cartoon) a pissed off Leaper, a small, rabbit-like creature that was a staple of Gaian diets.

Lisa giggled again, in the privacy of her helmet, at the memory of Peter rolling his eyes and informing Clone-a-tron, the magical device that only existed in the cartoon, "We're going to need another Tommy..."

On the screen the wolf had now cornered the rabbit, only

for the bunny to brandish a large can of baked beans, opening the lid with a savage jerk – before downing the contents in a single gulp. Lisa stepped closer, striving to be discrete and unobtrusive, as the Octopussy and his human friends laughed at the rabbit's expression of furious concentration – just before launching herself into the air with a mighty fart.

As Lisa drifted closer, a young man in a Jingcha's uniform glanced over at her. When she waved with her functional hand in a reassuring gesture, he looked back to the screen – just in time to watch the wolf gulping down a second can of beans. Only for the rabbit to drop a piece of lit kindling, the little piece of burning timber arriving just in time to ignite the wolf's fart. Everyone, including Lisa, laughed as the explosion turned the wolf into a pair of wide eyes in a blackened silhouette. Which then fell away, leaving a hairless wolf standing amidst a pile of burnt ash that had previously been his fur.

Next to the young man, a feminine colleague in uniform looked over at the towering, armored figure. "Did you need something?" she asked in the polite tones of a professional finding herself required to interact with a VIP from work during her personal time.

"I wanted to speak with Tako – after the show's over," Lisa hastily amended, before adding, "This is a funny show."

The Jingcha nodded, smiling in polite agreement, before turning back to face the screen.

As the cartoon played out, Lisa took the opportunity to not only enjoy the show, but to also watch Tako's reactions to what he was witnessing. The creature couldn't be expected to emulate human body language or vocalizations, but every time the wolf suffered an amusing injury the Octopussy's tentacles would... wriggle, slightly. Quivering, almost. Was that how Octopussies expressed amusement? Was that his laughter?

Here I am, playing at xenopsychology. She could only hope this wouldn't prove another dead end; Lisa was reduced to wild cards and desperate gambits at this point. Frankly, Lisa was beginning to feel a sense of sympathetic camaraderie towards the cartoon wolf. Who was, at that moment, fixated on a display in a desperate search for the RFID tag he'd slipped into a bowl of vegetables for the bunny to feast upon. His eyes swelled into two massive orbs larger than the rest of his head, then extended in cartoonishly phallic fashion to peer more closely at the display. Which was registering dozens, even hundreds of hits.

Then the wolf closed his – instantly normal sized – eyes, praying for mercy, as the massive warren of rabbits (all brandishing hunting rifles) moved in for the kill. The show ended with a scrolling screenshot of the rabbits in their hunting lodge, with a wolfskin rug laying before the fire. A rug which then lifted a paw to display a sign reading, *I should have gone to a steakhouse.*

The cartoon having ended, Tako's friends were free to give Lisa their undivided attention. Inside her armor the Huntress felt her usual social anxieties flaring; she reflexively began to deepen her breathing in response. *Deep breaths*. And while she breathed, she could size them up. Two men. Two women. *Couples?* Three of them were in uniform, but the second woman favored a warm looking turtleneck sweater. Dating one of the Jingchas, perhaps. Or just a friend with a different career path.

It was one of the men who spoke first. "Hey, Tako? We're going to go get some lunch. We'll see you later, okay?"

A tentacle rose from the surface of the tank, waving in

imitation of the human gesture. "Return as a friend or a fable," Tako declared in his high pitched synthetic voice.

As his human friends turned to leave, Lisa did her best to sear the words into her memory. *That* sounded like an utterance with strong cultural connotations! It didn't sound like any traditional farewell she had ever heard on any world, let alone Wigglebiggle. It was almost certainly the translator's interpretation of an Octopussy's parting sentiments that could provide insight into their mindset. *And that's exactly what I need.*

Lisa stepped closer to the tank, crouching slightly to put her helmeted visage on an even plane with Tako's massive eye. The two regarded each other in silence for a time, as the sapient invertebrate waited for Lisa to say something.

Crap. I should have had something prepared. She'd had plenty of time during the cartoon to come up with a few good questions to ask. "So..." Lisa began, then paused uncertainly. *Damn it. He's not even human.* She was no doubt damaging the reputation of her own species in his eyes. *I shouldn't be this shy around him.* "So... that was... a funny cartoon..." she managed, before mentally kicking herself. *That wasn't a question. Ask him a question!*

But apparently it had served as a probing statement, coaxing a response out of Tako. "I enjoy watching Briar Bunny," he declared in that childishly high pitched voice. "She's like an Octopussy that lost a few legs."

Lisa pondered that one for a few moments. The cartoon rabbit was certainly mischievous, much like Tako. Assuming of course that Tako represented something close to a baseline for his species. Lisa was groping in the dark, but at least she finally felt hopeful that she was beginning to move in the correct direction. More or less. Give or take. "So... how well did you know Ambassador Sashimi?" she asked. "I know I asked you that before, but could you tell me anything else about him?"

The invertebrate said nothing for several long moments. Was he thinking of what to say? Lisa glanced at the transparent walls of his tank. Tako's tentacles were moving slowly, which meant – if Chun were correct – that he was thinking, but not overly agitated. Lisa waited patiently for him to respond.

Finally, Tako provided some new information. "He was one year older than I am," he stated.

Again with the numbers? Twice now her questions about Sashimi had given her an answer involving statistics. Were the Octopussies particularly fond of mathematics? Then something else occurred to her. Tako's answer had been an obfuscation. It meant nothing by itself. "How old are *you*, Tako?" she asked.

Tako's tentacles wriggled slightly. Had he just played another joke on her? *Math themed humor.* "I am thirteen years old," Tako declared. His translator's voice synthesizer phrased it so flatly, as if he were neither boastful nor ashamed of it. And he'd already proven he knew how to make it extremely evocative, for the sake of his inhuman comedy routines.

So. He's thirteen. Is that adulthood for his species? "How long do Octopussies normally live?" the Huntress asked.

Tako's response was as flat and matter-of-fact as the last time. "Until we die."

Was that a joke? But his tentacles weren't quivering, which indicated he was being perfectly serious. *Or else I've misinterpreted that cue.* "How long does that usually take?" Lisa pressed him. *Yes, what **is** the lifespan of an Octopussy?* Thirteen years old – even on Wigglebiggle, whose orbit took slightly longer than the standard Federation year – was still decidedly juvenile for a human. Was Tako still considered a child by his species' standards?

It was something to ponder. And Lisa had plenty of time to ponder, because Tako was silent and his tentacles were swirling in the way that Chun had assured her meant the teenaged invertebrate was thinking of how to answer the question. Was he afraid to reveal that information?

Finally, Tako spoke up, his tone flat and devoid of teasing or emotion as he provided an answer. Of sorts. "I may have sixty friends around my age. Of my own kind." After allowing her a moment to process this seemingly unrelated piece of information, he continued on. "Last year I had over a hundred."

This is important. Lisa could *feel* it. She didn't feel as if she were floundering now. She felt as if she had found the equivalent of a urine mark. For a Gaian, such a scent was like a sign reading *Leaper ahead.* She was finally on the right track. *Forty friends lost in a single year.* "What happened to them?" she asked, feeling slightly euphoric with excitement.

"Most of them were eaten," Tako explained, and his synthesized voice remained flat and emotionless. Was he hiding his sentiments? Or... was his reaction something other than the grief a human would have felt?

Eaten. "By what?" she asked.

"Ask the perps I nicked," Tako advised.

The perps? The fishermen who'd attempted to poach. After a frozen moment, she blurted out in horror, "...They were *fished!?*"

Tako's tentacles swirled about in sudden excitement. Then he spoke again, adding an apologetic undertone to his clarification. "Some of them were eaten by things that the perps have caught," he explained. "Others were eaten by things that the perps have escaped from."

Escaped from. What horrors lay beneath the ocean surface? The Octopussies would know. And so would the fisherman, obviously. So, they weren't at the top of their food chain. As a Gaian, she understood that situation all too well. "I'm sorry for your loss," she said, trying to sound as sincere as possible.

Tako said nothing. Did he not understand the sentiment? Quite possibly. He was, after all, alien – truly alien, with an entire different psychology. *I'm a land dwelling primate. He's an oceanic mollusk.* She continued on, as much to cover her discomfiture at the awkward silence as anything else. "So most were eaten. What about the others?"

Now Tako's artificially generated voice held a trace of emotion. It sounded like... *pride*. "They were clever enough to find amusing deaths," he declared.

"Is an amusing death important?" she asked, even as her mind raced in confused fascination over the possibilities. For a human, getting oneself killed in an amusing fashion generally resulted in mockery from other humans for their display of stupidity. But to Octopussies, it was... *a badge of honor?*

A sudden flare burst inside her brain, and Lisa's eyes widened. A sudden epiphany as to the most probable culprit for the death of Ambassador Sashimi. *Could it really be that simple?* No. She had a prime suspect, but it defied her own belief. Her logic was leading her to a conclusion that was wildly improbable.

If you eliminate the impossible, then whatever remains – however improbable – must be the truth.

Gods. I really have become a Sherlock.

And then Tako delivered yet another thunderbolt of information, as he spoke up at last. "Every Octopussy is born with ten thousand brothers and sisters," he told her.

Ten. Thousand. *For each mating Octopussy.* Even if only a thousand of them reproduced in any given year, that would make for ten million progeny. The population growth would have been explosive.

No. Work it backwards. Sixty current siblings... no, just friends. *Assume them to be siblings, then extrapolate.* A loss of forty percent over the previous year. No doubt they were the most intelligent, or at least the luckiest, compared to the *thousands* of siblings that had died, most of them having likely died in their first year. *Now extrapolate.* If that were simply the current number of peers, rather than those specifically spawning from the same parentage as Tako...

*They are **not** the apex predators of their ecosystems.*

No wonder that Tako had admired the cartoon rabbit. He occupied the same place on his food chain!

"Humans..." Lisa gulped, feeling stunned by the revelation. "Humans usually only have one child at a time. And... and we expect the child to survive to adulthood."

"No wonder your sense of humor is so limited," Tako said.

Is he being serious about that? Lisa frowned suspiciously. Then her face cleared to an expression of wonderment, as she realized the answer. Even asking that question was alien to the Octopussies.

***Everything** is serious. And **everything** is to be laughed at!*

"Blasphemy," she murmured, dizzy with the revelations. "That's what you meant. Everything is a matter of life or death for you... and... and it's also all a joke..."

"Briar bunny is like an Octopussy," Tako said, in affirmation. "She knows the First Law: *no one ever gets out of life alive.*"

I've solved it. I know I have. No. She still needed *proof.* She *knew* she was right, but now she needed hard evidence to show to Patrick and the other colonists. "Thank... thank you, Tako," she stammered, trying to think of how to prove her theory beyond a reasonable doubt. "I... I have to go now. I hope you enjoy watching your cartoon."

"I hope you enjoy solving the case," Tako replied, in what Lisa now *knew* to be perfect sincerity.

The Huntress stumbled away, heading back towards the nearest entrance to the Gonganting. She was already beginning to formulate some possible proofs for her suspicions, but she was going to need a Watson for this.

Chapter 24

Lisa felt a bit uncomfortable about having the Chief Jingcha at her side, after the recent revelations. But this was about professionalism; she'd offered them so little of it that it seemed important to finish the investigation as properly as possible.

Besides, it would have been unseemly to simply accost a Jingcha and make demands, as opposed to making the request directly to the person in charge. And Jingcha Beatris looked harried enough as it was, given her responsibilities. "Yeah, we've got a few aquatic drones," she conceded, leaning against the edge of a workbench. Next to her, the eviscerated guts of a drone lay sprawled across the pockmarked surface, testimony to the work Lisa had interrupted. "We just haven't deployed any since the Octopussies said hello."

"And they have visual sensors like an Octopussy, correct?" Lisa inquired.

Beatris rolled her eyes, as much in annoyance as to look up at the Huntress' helmet, and the general location of her eyes. "Aye," she sighed. "The whole electromagnetic spectrum. Just like every other drone of the last few cen…" She shut her mouth abruptly and winced under Callan's fierce glare, before continuing in a less aggressive tone. "Plus sound, pressure, and other tactile readings."

Lisa was more than prepared to ignore the woman's attitude, at this point. She had dithered and been useless for an entire week, and now here she was making demands of someone who was obviously busy doing genuinely important work. This was Lisa's opportunity to redeem herself, after her succession of failures. "So can you modify a drone's settings to show a human the same visual spectrum as an Octopussy?" she asked.

Beatris frowned in sudden puzzlement, as she considered the notion. "That would be fairly easy," she conceded, reaching up with one hand to ruffle her unruly mane of fiery red hair. "But it wouldn't exactly show on a display. You'd have to be plugged into the drone. And you don't have one of these," she added, gently pulling at her forehead with her index finger and thumb. A slit appeared, spreading under the gentle tug to reveal the access port for the cybernetic implant that allowed Beatris to directly interface with mechanical devices as readily as her own appendages.

Lisa would have thought *crap* at that moment, except that she had already considered the issue. "Could you use the attachment point for a prosthetic limb?" she asked. Her left gauntlet drifted across her armored torso to rest thickly protected fingers against the surface of the smoothly polished cylinder that was her ubiquitous weapon. Her "gunhand," containing a myriad of useful devices ranging from a standard laser to the repurposed mining tool known as a *lightsaber*.

Beatris released her forehead and bit her knuckle instead, as she considered it. "It... would take some jury rigging," she conceded at last.

"How long will it take?" Lisa pressed her.

The Jingcha shrugged. "A couple of hours, maybe. If I get started right away."

"Do it," Callan snapped. "This takes priority."

"Yes, ma'am," sighed Beatris, with the typical annoyance of a harried worker who, while halfway through a task deemed of immediate and vital importance by her supervisor, has just been handed another task and been told the same thing once more.

"Thank you," Lisa said, adding in perfect sincerity, "I very much appreciate it." Then, before she could think (and give her self-doubts an opportunity to stop her), she deliberately rushed to add, "um, Chun? While we wait, could you come with me?"

The Chief Jingcha arched an eyebrow. "What is it?"

Lisa was already in motion, not daring to look at the woman. She could already feel her pulse quickening with nervous trepidation. But it was time for some honesty. She *owed* it to the woman. "I want to talk to you in private. We can go to the quarters you assigned me."

Then Lisa moved out of the room, too quickly to notice the soft intake of breath. Or to notice the eagerness with which Callan followed. Or perhaps she was deliberately ignoring it, lest she lose her resolve.

Chapter 25

Chun felt as nervous and giddy as a schoolgirl on a first date, as the door shut behind her. Alone at last with the Huntress herself. Of course it wasn't exactly intimate, not with her still in that overpowering exoskeleton. The modified XTMP-III was well suited to its role in protecting the wearer from all manner of energies and physical impacts, but it wasn't exactly meant for intimate moments. Chun had been pining to get a good look at the Huntress, in the flesh, without the bulky armor to neuter her beauty.

Then she heard the soft hiss of vacuum tight seals being released, and her throat went dry. She watched with widening eyes as the armor split open along its seams like a cocoon, from which its occupant could squirm free. She bit her lip and waited politely, even as her heart began to race with anticipation.

The Huntress looked even more glorious in the flesh than she had in the recordings and images Chun had managed to get her hands on. Images alone couldn't quite capture the breathtaking stature of the woman, the way she loomed. Recordings didn't impart the scent of the dried sweat from having essentially *lived* in that armor for days on end, to the point that her green tresses were plastered flat to her scalp. The way her muscles rippled under the short sleeved bodysuit that hugged her contours and emphasized her overpowering majesty.

The amazonian beauty strode towards the desk in utter silence, as Chun watched in mute admiration. A hand like an industrial vice encased in silk snatched up the prosthetic laying there, as the Huntress attached her limb with the automatic reflexes of an amputee who'd had years to grow accustomed to its presence. Stiff fingers like those of a statue twitched and flexed, taking on the appearance of living flesh. All while Chun looked on and hungered.

Finally the looming Huntress spoke, while keeping her gaze fixated on the far corner of the room, where the floor met the walls. "Is it..." She hesitated, then began again, her voice only slightly higher pitched than what came out through her suit's speakers. "Is it true that you... desire me?"

Chun's cheeks flushed scarlet, and she flinched with the humiliation of discovery. *Patrick told her!* She was going to break her old friend's arm, and maybe a leg, when she caught a hold of him next! As it was, she could only nod her head in silent mortification. Then, realizing the woman probably couldn't see it, she squeaked out a verbal affirmation. "Yeah... uh... yeah."

The Huntress continued to stare at the floor, carefully not looking at Chun for several long moments. The silence began to feel oppressive, before Chun's crush spoke up. "I'm sorry."

Chun blinked, then gulped. "I... for what?"

The Huntress folded her arms over her chest and sighed. Even with her limbs in the way, Chun couldn't help but stare admiringly at that swelling bosom encased in that bodysuit. "I thought you wanted to... arrest me. Or something," the amazonian figure confessed, still staring at the floor.

Chun blinked again, now thoroughly confused. "Why would I want to do that?" she wondered, taking a step closer, angling for a glimpse of the younger, taller woman's face. Then she realized those arms weren't actually folded over each other. The Huntress was... hugging herself. And her expression looked more sad, than anything.

And when she spoke, Chun could hear the sadness in her voice. "I don't... I don't really see myself as being attractive," Lisa explained, still staring at the floor. "When people look at me, I think they're scared of me. They think I'm a monster. And... I can't really blame them."

"You don't look like a monster," Chun insisted, taking a slow, careful step closer yet.

"I feel like one, though," Lisa sighed, before adding, "And... sometimes I act like one. I have a... a body count. A big one."

Chun felt the need to testify on Lisa's own behalf. "I've seen your record. I know what kind of people you deal with. It's not as if your kills weren't justified."

"Sometimes they are," Lisa sighed, biting her lip. "Sometimes, I..." She shut her eyes, shaking her head vigorously. "Sometimes, I kill them because I enjoy it. I get so caught up on how *righteous* it feels, and I... I've never taken any prisoners, did you know that?"

"Yeah. I know that," Chun agreed, before adding, "Except for that one guy. From... Golden Ruler, wasn't it?"

"Golden Rule," Lisa corrected her. "And that was more like a kidnapping, if I'm being honest."

Chun considered it. "You're an FIA operative," she pointed out. "If it were a problem, they wouldn't have hired you."

"That's because I'm a stalking goat for the damned Overone," Lisa protested, lifting her head to glare at Chun. Her eyes opened – and Chun was staring into two glowing orbs like stars in the night sky.

The eyes. Those Gaian eyes. The microevolutionary adaptation to the forest understory. Chun knew about them, but that wasn't the same thing as *seeing* them. Feeling their gaze, like two targeting beams locking onto her face. She shivered.

"Sorry," Lisa breathed, sharply turning her head away.

"Don't be. I liked it," Chun murmured, her cheeks flushed. "I... Patrick told you I read your file, right? I know all about it. All of it. Did... did you ever find out what happened to Romeo, afterwards?"

Lisa shook her head, silently staring at the wall.

Chun took a deep breath, then exhaled with a huff. "Right. Well, I looked into it. He's now in a cohabitation contract with Adra Agrippina. I'd say it worked out pretty well. You... you did good, okay?"

"I kidnapped a man and returned him to his estranged lover, because she paid me," Lisa pointed out.

"And now they both look pretty happy together," Chun countered. She leaned against the desk, allowing her to look at Lisa's face despite how she was turned away from her. "Nobody arrested you for kidnapping. Or murder. Nobody's going to, okay? Certainly not me."

Lisa sighed, shaking her head ruefully. "So you don't want me in shackles, huh?" she muttered wryly.

Chun shivered, then hissed through her teeth. "We could take turns," she offered gallantly.

Lisa opened her eyes and stared straight at the wall, her cheeks flushing in her own embarrassed reaction. "Wow," she gulped. "I... that's quite the offer," she managed.

Chun stared up at the woman's face, and began to feel deflated. "You're not interested," she groaned in resignation.

"I... I never even thought about it, to be honest," Lisa confessed, finally turning to face her. As she lowered her arms and exposed her chest, Chun found herself presented with those massive mounds at eye level. They jiggled ever so slightly as their bearer spoke. "I thought of you as... the Chief Jingcha. Not as anything... else."

"Story of my life," Chun sighed, slumping against the desk and trying not to sink into a funk.

"You must have had other partners before," Lisa suggested. "I mean... you *are* attractive..."

"No such luck," Chun grumbled. "I'm the big, bad Chief. I was the big, bad Chief before I was even the Chief."

"Yeah." Lisa turned to press her muscular rump against the desk, slumping against it next to Chun in a show of camaraderie. "I know how that one feels."

Chun shook her head. In a wistful tone, she murmured, "I just... I was hoping to meet someone who I didn't grow up with. It's hard to feel sexy around someone who remembers when your front baby teeth fell out."

Lisa frowned, then pointed out, "I *am* younger than you are. You could have tried someone too young to have seen..."

"*That* would mean the *child* of someone who knew me without my front baby teeth," Chun cut her off. "No, thank you." After a moment, she added, "I know what happened to you on New Athens. I'm sorry about that... but..."

"Sorry for what part?" Lisa asked. There was the slightest edge to her voice. "Sorry for looking into my private life? Or sorry for what happened to me?"

Chun checked her psyche for signs of guilt. "I'm not sorry for doing my homework, if that's what you're thinking," she retorted. "But I'm sorry that you got your heart broken.

And..." She couldn't help but be honest, "I guess I'm sorry that I felt kinda glad about it. It meant you were... um... available."

"Thanks," Lisa grumbled ruefully.

They sat together in silence for a time, before Chun asked, "so... *are* you available?" Then she mentally kicked herself, before hunching her shoulders and looking down at the floor. The head of the colony's law enforcement agency waited miserably to be shot down once again.

Lisa said nothing at first. Then she murmured, "...am I? I'm not actually sure."

Chun looked up at her, surprised by the answer.

Lisa shrugged, then said, "I've been spending time on Furcadia."

Chun tried to focus on the words, and not the way the shrug made Lisa's chest jiggle. "That's the planet of transhumans, right?"

"Yeah," Lisa nodded.

Chun frowned, then tilted her head. "I've heard they're pretty... licentious," she ventured.

"That's a pretty good way to put it," Lisa conceded. "They tend towards polyamory, and casual... you know."

"Sex," Chun murmured. Lisa flushed beet red, but nodded. "So... you've met someone," Chun ventured on.

"Several someones," Lisa admitted. "I'm not sure if we're just friends, or there's something more going on."

"Maybe you should ask?" Chun suggested.

Lisa grimaced, then nodded. "Yeah. We're probably just friends, but I should check to make sure."

Chun glanced away, then looked back at Lisa. "So... where does that leave us?"

Lisa stared at the floor, then glanced at Chun's legs. They were both seated on the edge of the desk, but Chun's boots were kicking lightly in the air. A sharp contrast to how Lisa's heels were firmly pressed into the floor. Chun could see Lisa staring at the difference in the lengths of their limbs. "Yeah, I'm pretty short," she grumbled, acknowledging the unspoken observation.

Lisa coughed delicately, still staring at Chun's booted feet. "You're... I guess I'd say... cute? If I weren't afraid of pissing you off, I mean," she managed, with a strained smile at her own attempt at humor.

Chun felt her face grow hot. "You think I'm cute?" she whispered, her heart beginning to pound.

Lisa gulped and risked a glance at Chun's face, before hastily looking away. "Well... yeah. Sure. I mean, you're in great shape, and then there's your voice..."

"What about my voice?" Chun wondered aloud.

"Well..." Lisa hesitated, before picking words with obvious care. "It's the... the cadence, I guess you could say. You make everything sound like it's a command. All authority. Like a..." She shut her mouth suddenly, biting her lip.

"Like a what?" Chun asked, frowning suspiciously.

Lisa coughed delicately. "I... I was going to say... like a... like a parent. But I didn't want to... um..."

"Oh," Chun grunted. "I don't suppose you meant like one of those mythological parents? The ones who were always getting it on with their kids?"

"I mean, kind of?" Lisa shrugged. "You make everything sound like, if I just do whatever you say, everything's going to be okay. It feels... comforting." She sighed and carefully did not look at Chun. "Sorry if that sounds bad."

"No. No, it sounds... flattering, I guess," Chun conceded. Then, after a moment to consider it, she added, "I like your voice too. It's so deep and husky. It's like... a bedroom voice."

Lisa burst out into a sharp bark of sudden laughter. "Oh, come on!" she guffawed, shaking her head.

"No, I'm serious," Chun insisted. "You always sound like you just rolled out of bed, after a fun time."

Lisa laughed again, shaking her head in amused disbelief at the praise. "I always thought I sounded too much like a man," she pined ruefully. "I sing bass. When I try singing, I mean."

Chun grinned impishly in sudden mischievous inspiration. "Should I command you to sing for me?" she teased.

"Oh!" Lisa grunted, then lowered her head. After a moment her chest began to shake with her helpless laughter. Chun let herself join in, and the two women laughed together.

Finally, when they had fallen silent and caught their breath, Chun sighed. "So... where does that leave us?" she asked.

Lisa considered it, occasionally taking cautious glances in Chun's direction. "To be honest...?" she ventured.

Chun bit her lip nervously, waiting in wary dread of the answer.

"To be honest," Lisa sighed. "I... I could really use friends, more than anything."

Chun did her best to hide the sudden pain in her chest. "Uh... you don't mean like a Furcadian friend, do you?" She couldn't help but add a hopeful tinge to her voice.

For her part, Lisa seemed oblivious. "I'm not even sure," she confessed. "I really do need to check in with Jenny, and Brutus and Harvey. I don't want to do anything before I know if it'd be honorable or not."

"That... that sounds fair..." Chun conceded. Then, after realizing Lisa hadn't actually clarified it, she asked, "So, if they *do* say it's okay...?"

"Then I still want to be friends," Lisa replied. But she was smiling as she said it. "Furcadian friends, maybe. I... I think I do like you, Chun."

Chun felt the elation soar in her chest. "I like you too," she breathed, sudden excitement rushing through her system.

"Yeah. I think I got that," Lisa murmured wryly. "Um... so you prefer women?" she asked. Then she frowned in sudden suspicion. "Or is it that I look enough like a man to...?" Her expression twisted with sudden self-doubts.

"I like them both," Chun grunted. "Remember Nushi? The woman whose daughter sold the Varuna rolls?" At Lisa's wary nod of affirmation, she went on. "She was my first girlfriend."

"Oh." After a moment, Lisa asked, "so what happened?"

"She decided she liked boys more than girls," Chun sighed. "Or at least, she liked a boy more than this girl. He's been a good husband to her," she added, lest she sound jealous.

Lisa nodded, then murmured a sympathetic, "ouch."

"Yeah. Ouch," Chun agreed. "So... about those... Jenny, you called her?"

"And Brutus, and Harvey," Lisa said. Then a strange expression came over her face, before she suggested in a hopeful tone of voice, "Did you want to... hear about them? Maybe see some pictures? You might like them..."

Chun closed her eyes and sighed deeply. Then she exhaled sharply, opening her eyes wide and setting her expression in a determined smile. "You know what? Yeah, why not?" she said, accepting the offer. "We've got some time to kill, before Beatris has everything ready. In the meantime, you can tell me all about them."

Lisa smiled shyly, and the expression made Chun feel as if her heart were singing.

Chapter 26

"Okay. Strap yourself in."

Lisa stared at the Gonganting's senior drone technician in some bemusement. "I beg your pardon?" she gulped, her anxieties flaring at the prospect of having her limbs immobilized while blinded and deafened to whatever might be going on in her personal proximity.

Beatris gestured at the straps hanging from one side of the operator's chair. "The safety harness. Strap yourself in."

Lisa's anxieties were dancing a mad rhythm in her head, something with a heavy emphasis on percussion instruments. "Is that really necessary?" she asked, giving Chun a beseeching glance.

"It's for your own protection," Beatris shot back, even as she reached for a roll of duct tape. This did little to defuse Lisa's fears. But Beatris continued on, in a voice of impatient reasonableness, "Look. When you're hooked up, sometimes the body flails around. Like sleep walking. So it's just to keep you from yanking things out without meaning to." She thrust the duct tape downward, gesturing at the lower region of the chair. "See the sleeves for your feet? You can slip them in and out, when you actually want to. Same as on the armrests."

"Oh," Lisa nodded, managing a weak grin. Then, in perhaps a sharper tone than she'd intended, she demanded, "then what's with the duct tape?"

Beatris waggled the roll from side to side. "You wanted me to route the feed through a prosthetic limb attachment point. Your arm ends at the elbow, right? That means I'll need to tape your bicep down, so you don't yank the cord out."

Lisa felt her cheeks growing beet red. "I... couldn't you just hook the cord up through my cyberlimb?"

Beatris gave a great, heaving sigh of frustration and annoyance. "Look, you wanted me to jury rig it through your attachment. That's tricky enough, without having to run it through another device. As it is, I'm not going to be held responsible if you start tasting the things you touch after this."

"Is that a thing!?" Lisa yelped, beginning to panic.

"It's called synesthesia. It happens sometimes, when you're messing around with neural links. Now either strap in or stop wasting my time," Beatris growled.

Deep breaths. Lisa chided herself, as she began to gulp for air. *Deep breaths. You can do this. They **need** you to do this.* Her eyes rolled and roamed about the room, before settling on where Chun watched with her usual expression of weary calm. The Chief Jingcha saw Lisa looking at her, and that placid expression shifted into an encouraging smile. One that Lisa now knew represented hopeful admiration.

Call it what it is. I've got a fangirl.

A fangirl old enough to be her mother, at that. Not that the woman's age was a problem. *I could use a motherly hug, right about now.* Especially from someone who Lisa now knew held her in such high esteem.

That was the thought that pulled Lisa through her anxiety attack. Chun was her fan. Chun was watching her own personal hero. *I mustn't disappoint her.* Chun still believed in her. Even if Lisa had trouble believing in herself, she could still care about not disappointing someone who did in fact believe in her.

Once the harness was clicked into place and her feet slipped into the loops of elastic cloth meant for them, Lisa nodded acceptingly towards Beatris. "Okay. Tape me, and then... tell me how I'm supposed to control the drone."

Beatris' loud bark of laughter elicited another flush from Lisa, this one born from humiliation. "It takes a *lot* of training before you can control drones with a VR rig. And that's when you *have* an actual control rig. You don't." She pointed at her own forehead by way of illustration. "I'll be hooked up right next to you, and you'll be slaved on my feed."

Lisa's throat felt tight as she swallowed hard. She dared not even look in Chun's direction. *A slave to the woman who just tied me up. I want to be back in my armor.* Her attempt at "eccentricity" was beginning to seem less foolish than it had a few minutes ago.

But the colony needed her to confirm her theory, and Chun needed to see her hero in action. Lisa focused on her breathing as Beatris slipped into the chair next to her, strapping herself in and feeding the plug of a cable into her forehead. "You'll want to close your eyes for this," Beatris advised, as she slipped her hands into the sleeves on her armrests. "It'll make the shift a little less confusing."

Lisa shut them tightly. *Deep breaths.*

"Okay. Now you can open them."

Lisa opened her eyes. And suddenly she understood why some people took psychedelic drugs for recreational purposes.

The colors!

She couldn't even describe them. And not just because she didn't seem to have a mouth anymore. There were colors she had never had a frame of reference for, that she couldn't have described beyond a vague "three hues past violet," or "a couple of hues before you get to red."

"Can you tell me if you're doing okay?" Beatris' voice rang in her head. Lisa wanted to respond, but that was proving to be difficult without a mouth. "Here. Let me try this," Beatris hummed.

Suddenly Lisa felt as if a mouth had formed, somewhere on the strange nothingness where her face had been. "I'm doing amazing," she declared. "It's... it's all so beautiful. I mean, I can't feel anything. I feel like I have eyes but not a face. Or a body. But what I'm seeing, it... it's..."

"Yeah," Beatris agreed, with a husky purr to her voice. "This is why I love my job." And Lisa's vision drifted, her field of view moved as the drone they were connected to swam through the waters beneath the docks. "You see those? Those long ribbons we're cutting through?"

"Oh gods. It's like we're pushing through rainbows," Lisa gasped.

"That's the seaweed we eat. Looks a lot different like this, doesn't it?" Beatris cooed, as they drifted past what had looked like dark green tendrils and leaves to human eyes.

"Is this what you do all day?" Lisa murmured, utterly incredulous.

"Why do you think I was pissed about the interruption? I was fixing up one of my favorite aerial drones." Beatris was taking them out of the patch of seaweed, and now the vastness of the ocean stretched out before them. Lisa could see it all, a wide variety of shapes and sizes to the life forms swimming or floating through the water. Some of it looked utterly terrifying. Her own eyes were adapted for close range visual detail; the drone's sensors were sharp enough to make out the vaguest hints of large bodies in the deeper ocean. Many of them appeared to be predatory in their movements.

"Can you take us towards the hydroelectric plant?" Lisa asked, as much to avoid getting any closer to the monstrous things out in the depths as to achieve her intended purpose. "Wigglebiggle Hydroelectric Plant Number Three?"

"Sure. You want to get near the turbine they found the body in?" Beatris asked, even as the drone began to pick up speed, swimming more swiftly through the coastal waters.

"Yeah," Lisa breathed, as she enjoyed the passing view. Even the sand glittered like tiny gemstones, an entire beach of underwater treasures below her. A school of small, swift looking fish, their scales shimmering hypnotically as their movements kept changing the way the light reflected off them, swam past them.

Suddenly a long tentacle, tipped with a mouth consisting of three jaws arranged symmetrically like a three fingered claw, shot out from a tubelike structure nestled in the sand. The worm-like creature seized one of the fish in its razor sharp teeth, coiling around it as it brought its prey down to enjoy. The entire school darted away in unison, the collective of fish fleeing the predator that had claimed one of their own. Another tentacle shot out, as if it had been waiting on their predictable reaction. This tentacle was lined with suckers along its length. An Octopussy's limb. One of the other seven made a show of waving at the passing drone in a friendly fashion, while the rest helped to slip the fish into its beak.

Lisa silently wished it a happy feasting. Then she was admiring other sights. Things that looked like shelled mollusks, their glittering shields waving in the current like the seaweed as the water let nutrients flow to them. Then she suppressed a yelp as she caught sight of what looked to be, at first glance, a BEM skittering across the ocean floor.

No. It doesn't have enough limbs for a BEM. It had a multitude, certainly, but it lacked the sheer nightmarish quality of the perennial pests. It did however have two large, impressive looking claws on its frontal limbs, and a tail trailing behind it. *Is that a Varuna lobster?* It wasn't the only one of its kind that she could see, but they were milling about independently rather than forming a coordinated supply chain back to a central hive. Most likely the lobsters, then.

"Here we are," Beatris informed her, as the drone turned to steer closer to the turbine. It loomed slightly with its size and distinctive appearance, the pipe's artificial nature a sharp contrast to the terrifying beauty of the ocean.

"Can you get us a look inside?" Lisa asked. "Where the ambassador was killed?"

"Sure thing," drolled Beatris, as their shared view began to move into the turbine itself.

Can the drone fit inside? Or is it extending the optical sensor? Either way, Lisa was beginning to get a good look at... *beauty*.

That was the only way to describe it. Beauty. It *was* beauty. It was the most accurate physical representation of the very concept of beauty that Lisa had never imagined could ever have existed. It didn't just glitter. It *shimmered* in a kaleidoscopic fashion. It was like diamonds cut into prisms. Prisms that spun around and made rainbows shine and twirl about like dancers. Dancing rainbows making love atop diamonds.

She couldn't look away. She didn't want to look away. All she wanted to do was to go on looking at Beauty incarnate, forever. They were coming closer to Beauty, drifting closer to Beauty itself...

Lisa gave a shocked, guttural gasp and stared at the far

wall, feeling half-blind. The muted, *ugly* colors of her own vision were blurred through tears of pain and grief as she shook violently from the sudden jerk back to her own reality.

Next to her, Beatris was sobbing quietly, making incoherent little noises.

"I need a medical team in here! **Now!**" screamed Chun, her bellowing voice gone as frantic with terror as it was commanding.

She's scared for us, Lisa dimly registered. *For... me?* She gulped and tried to make her mouth form words, but they wouldn't come out. She sounded as incoherent as Beatris. She would have felt more frightened if she didn't recognize this feeling. *It's like a concussion. I don't think I've damaged anything. I'll recover in a little bit. I just need to rest and recover.*

Hands were grabbing at her, as the medical personnel began to ply their trade. Several strong looking men in uniform were taking hold of her limbs, their fingers digging into parts of her anatomy that she would normally have felt violated to have manhandled in such a fashion. For some reason Lisa didn't feel particularly upset about it. The men looked attractive. Strong bodies and faces that shone with compassionate intentions towards her person. *I really like that one.* Would Chun like to team up on him? *No, he's too young for her. Maybe. She's really missing out.*

Then it occurred to her that she ordinarily wouldn't be smiling so flirtatiously at a man who was hauling her with his colleagues and placing her onto a stretcher. *It's probably the concussion talking. I hope I don't feel too embarrassed when I'm myself again.*

Chun was walking alongside the stretcher as the men brought her into the hall. "It'll be okay," she half declared, half prayed, her eyes wide with terrified concern.

It's okay, Chun. Lisa wanted to chide her. *Shouldn't you be checking on that sexy redhead back there?* Knowing she wasn't thinking like her usual self didn't help. Possibly because Lisa was enjoying feeling this way.

Everybody's sexy. Even I'm sexy. And I'm Sherlock Holmes.

"Let's get an IV into her." The voice was calm despite the tenseness in the atmosphere. Whoever it was doing the speaking, he sounded as if he were addressing Chun. "It looks like pretty standard dump shock. They should both be fine in a day or two."

"Dump shock," Lisa slurred, as she finally managed to convince her mouth to cooperate with her. "Hot..."

"Hot? Are you feeling hot?" the voice asked, suddenly concerned about unusual symptoms. A pair of big, beautiful eyes poking over the top of a medical mask stared down at her. Over the doctor's shoulder, Chun was staring down and looking wretched with concern.

"Naw..." Lisa slurred, focusing her pathetically *human* eyes upon the Chief Jingcha's face. "Yer hot. Chun. You... yer hot..." Lisa's body shook slightly, as a sudden giggle escaped. "And I'm Sherlock Holmes..."

Chun stared down at Lisa, then gave the doctor a look of utter anguish. "Is... is that brain damage? Is she damaged?" she demanded fearfully.

"Naw. I'll be fine... just... con... concussed..." Lisa assured her. "Felt this... before. Not this bad... but I'll be fine. Tell her, doc..."

The doctor was glancing at something Lisa couldn't see. Most likely a display for whatever devices he had monitoring her. "It certainly looks that way," he concurred. "She should be fine with some rest. At least one day of total bed rest. I'll need to check on Beatris."

"Check... Beatris... yeah..." Lisa agreed. "Chun... stay..."

The doctor drifted away to focus his attention on his

other patient, as Chun stepped closer, reaching out to feel for Lisa's hand. "I... I'm here..." the Chief Jingcha stammered, clutching tightly at Lisa's fingers.

"I did it," Lisa grinned, staring up at her face. "I did it. I'm Sherlock Holmes."

Chun blinked. The reassurances that it was a simple concussion were somewhat less than believable, given the apparent ravings. "What... what are you talking about?" she quavered.

"Solved... the case..." Lisa chuckled. Then, through sheer force of will, she managed to curl her fingers around Chun's. "I'm Sherlock Holmes. Yer my Watson. And... and yer *hot*... friends... Furcadian..."

Chun blinked. Then she grinned and nodded, squeezing Lisa's thick fingers with both hands now.

Chapter 27

Of course there was no way Lisa would have done this without her armor. She had finally unwound enough to allow Chief Jingcha Callan – Chun – to see her outside of her protective shell, and of course the medical staff at the colony's capital hospital now had intimate knowledge of her body, both inside and out. *But one step at a time.* She wasn't about to engage in public speaking with mere fabric between her and an entire roomful of listeners.

*And not just the ones **in** the room, either.*

Lisa had already asked what representatives from the Octopussies would be present, while resting in the hospital with neurosensors pressed to her scalp and anesthetics flowing through her blood. Governor Patrick Chu – who had been quick to rush over and check on both his contractor, and the injured Jingcha in the room next door – had had to clarify that there didn't seem to be any form of hierarchal behavior evidenced by the Octopussies. "We do know that they have at least a few societal customs," he had continued, while Chun had helped Lisa to feed herself. "And it's because they don't actually die, unless they're killed."

Lisa had felt uncertain and worried after hearing that. It had confused her. More pertinently, it had left her worrying about possible brain damage from the dump shock incurred during her experience with the aquatic drone. But thankfully Patrick had clarified. "They don't die of old age. I don't know about diseases, but otherwise they live until something kills them. And... they get a little bigger every year."

Lisa had felt a little less uncertain after hearing that clarification. "Giants in the deep," she had muttered, and then slurped another mouthful of noodles.

"Yep," Patrick confirmed, before going on to recount what was now referred to as First Contact for the species. An infamous event that had taken place the previous year, after rumors of a series of events and unsettling incidents had reached the ears of relevant Federation officials. Incidents that caused them to suspect the existence of sapient aquatic life. *Previously undetected sapient life*. "The Federation investigation team put their ship on hover above the ocean, and sent down a probe on a cable. It went down... oh, about three, maybe four kilometers... and then a giant tentacle grabbed it."

Lisa had munched on noodles and listened with interest, despite the headache from her injuries. "It shook the probe like a rattle," Patrick had continued, while she ate. "Then it tied the cable in knots... and then..." Patrick paused, frowning at the recollection. "And then it gave the entire thing a sharp *yank*." He snorted, shaking his head in wry amusement. "Probably would have pulled the ship under, if they hadn't detached the cable."

"So what happened to the probe?" Lisa had asked.

"A couple of smaller Octopussies returned it. Dumped it on the docks like they were tossing out garbage."

"So that's what convinced everyone the Octopussies were sapient," Lisa mused.

"Well, that and the knots in the line. Perfect bowline on a bight."

The memory of that conversation was less than a day old, when Lisa lurched into the conference room to finish the job she had been hired to perform. Her head was still aching, and even the painkillers could only do so much, but she didn't want to wait any longer for her moment of triumph. *My denouement. I'm actually getting to have a denouement, like Sherlock Holmes!* Her migraine could wait.

Governor Chu was present, of course. Patrick was waiting with his hands steepled on the table and an intent expression on his face. Naturally so; he had been desperate to save his colony, his world, from involuntary migration in accordance with Federation law. *And I've saved his world for him.* Chun was there as well, sitting next to him and looking stiff and formal in her uniform. But her eyes were shining, and now Lisa knew that it was admiration in those eyes, gleaming at her so intently. *I've validated her belief in me.* Director Astrid Stuart was present as well, along with the heads of the other hydroelectric facilities, and other assorted representatives of the colony's government.

There was also a terminal on the desk next to the Governor, and as she entered the room Patrick spoke up. "Are you ready on your end?" he inquired.

From the terminal there came a voice that even a bass singer would have considered to be shockingly deep. It positively rumbled in the bones, sending vibrations up and down the spine. A voice that could be authentically described as *primordial*. It was the voice of an elder god that appeared in the nightmares of artists. It was the voice of an entity that had slumbered for eons, that had been worshiped by creatures that had gone extinct before the rise of humanity.

"I have been waiting for this. For a very long time."

Lisa glanced around the room, curious to see the reactions of everyone present. Patrick was looking even more stiffly nervous than before. Chun frowned faintly. Most of the others present were evidencing varying levels of discomfiture. A god had spoken from beneath the waves, and they were feeling all the more reminded that they were intruders on an alien world.

For her part, Lisa was fighting off a smirk, even if nobody could see it through the obscuring confines of her helmet. "I know you're doing that on purpose," she declared, unable to hide the amusement in her voice.

"I'm trying to play the part," the elder Octopussy freely admitted. "**I am the eldritch entity from the deep. The Old One who slumbers beneath the waves**."

Of course they did. Of course the Octopussies learned about H.P Lovecraft. "Sure thing, Cthulhu," Lisa chuckled. Around the room, the supervisors responsible for the colony's electrical power, sanitation, and other vital infrastructure traded uncertain glances and attempted to recover their composure.

"Have I just been given a name?" asked the booming voice.

Crap. This was her big moment, but she didn't want to screw it up by insulting the creature. "That depends," she vacillated. "Do you like it?"

"It is sufficiently grand for a being such as myself," decreed the creature.

"All right, then. It's a pleasure to meet you, Cthulhu," Lisa replied. She took another glance around the room, then braced herself. *Deep breaths. This is your moment.* "I know who killed Ambassador Sashimi," she announced.

Patrick was looking tense enough to shatter like glass, as he braced himself. Chun – who had already heard Lisa's theory, and watched her confirm it – merely smiled. The others braced themselves for the big revelation.

Lisa took another deep breath, determined not to stammer, slur her words, or let her voice crack, as she finally revealed the truth behind the mystery.

"Sashimi killed Sashimi."

Chun, having already heard Lisa's explanation while sitting vigil by her hospital bed, continued to smile. For everyone else, the announcement elicited an assortment of variations of a singular monosyllable. *Huh?*

"An Octopussy's visual range is far wider than that of a human's," Lisa went on, as she began her explanation, walking them through what must have happened. "They can see colors that humans don't. The turbines are composed of materials that... glitter, to an Octopussy. Especially when they're running, when they're... spinning..." Lisa trailed off and closed her eyes, as the memory of Beauty itself came to her once more.

Then she forced herself to concentrate on the discussion taking place, between Director Stewart and a colleague from another hydroelectric plant. "If the turbine were in use, there might have been a kaleidoscopic effect," they mused thoughtfully.

"Sashimi must have simply... slithered into the turbine, in search of the Beauty," Lisa sighed. She shut her eyes again, as the memory came back to her. *I can't blame him*. She would be keeping that memory in her head for a very long time.

"We are... so sorry..." Patrick declared, in an anguished tone. Lisa opened her eyes, taking in his guilt-wracked expression. "I can assure you, Cthulhu, we'll be taking steps to prevent another tragedy like this one..."

"**That will *not* be necessary**," the self-styled elder god interrupted the Governor.

Lisa could *feel* the tension in the air, even through her armor. It was time for the verdict, and now their entire colony's fate rested on the natives' judgment of humanity. Everyone present was terrified, nervous to the point of panic. Lisa knew the feeling – but not from dread of the verdict. Her usual social discomfiture aside, she already *knew* what Cthulhu was about to say.

"**Humanity has proven themselves**," the primordial entity from beneath the waves declared. "**We, the Octopussies, are ready to join your Federation**."

Another frozen moment passed, before the information sank into the minds of those present. Then the tension melted away, as groans of relief and delighted chuckles reverberated. Director Stuart was actually hugging someone else, and everyone was grinning. And Governor Chu was lurching to his feet and bowing at the waist, aiming the top of his skull at Lisa in a formal gesture of deepest respect and gratitude. "You... you've saved us... you've saved my world..." he began to gush. The tears were already beginning to leak from his eyes. "You helped us prove our good intentions..."

"I helped you prove you can be entertaining," Lisa interrupted him in mid-gush.

Patrick froze. Then he straightened up. Then he turned his head to stare at the terminal in silence.

"**You have indeed proven yourselves**," Cthulhu agreed. "**Humans are *very* entertaining**."

Patrick stared at the terminal for a long moment. Then his cheeks began to flush beet red. His eyes bulged, his adam's apple bobbed as he swallowed hard. Then he made a noise that might have been Mandarin, or simply a brief utterance of disbelieving Angrish.

"Did it never occur to you that we have no way to force you to leave?" Cthulhu pointed out. **"You are aliens from the stars, with powers beyond our imagining. You breathe out of water. But the moment we first learned of you, we knew it would be entertaining."**

"Buhuh?" Patrick replied, still red faced and looking as if he might keel over. There was a faint throbbing in his temple, from a blood vessel pulsing beneath the surface.

"We never wanted the humans to leave in the first place," Cthulhu informed him. **"We simply wanted to see what you would do."**

"So that's why you sent an ambassador," Lisa said accusingly. "You knew it was only a matter of time before Sashimi would find an interesting death, and start the... entertainment."

"I never sent anyone," Cthulu insisted. **"Nobody did."**

Lisa stared at the terminal, uncertain if Cthulhu had any sort of visual feed to go with the audio. Then she glanced at the red faced Governor.

Thankfully, Patrick had slumped back into his chair, before the developing aneurysm could burst. "We... we never thought to check for credentials," he admitted, staring at nothing. "Why would we? It... I just..."

"Octopussies have never shown any indication of hierarchal activity," Chun reminded him. She reached out and placed a gentle hand on his shoulder, touching him reassuringly.

"So... so he wasn't an ambassador..." Patrick whimpered, still staring straight ahead with a dull, unseeing expression. "He was just... some guy. Some guy with... with tentacles. Who swam up and lied about being an ambassador."

Lisa checked the reactions of everyone else present. *Bemusement* appeared to be the prevailing sentiment. A few individuals were sharing muttered whispers, though none of them seemed to be interested in contributing to the general discussion.

Patrick finally shut his eyes, his face scrunching up as he groaned. "The Octopussies are laughing at us. Aren't they." It was not a question.

"**You have been *very* entertaining**," Cthulhu confirmed.

Patrick sighed, his eyes still closed. "Great. So. What happens now?"

"**Now? Now I make my proclamation, for all the galaxy to witness**." Cthulhu paused for a moment for dramatic effect. And Lisa couldn't help but reflect on just how *intelligent* the Octopussies were. The alien had never even seen a human in the flesh. It lived at the bottom of the ocean, having grown too large from having lived for so long. And yet it was able to not only decode the language of beings so wildly different from itself, but to have also mastered pitch and timing, like a professional speaker.

Or a comedian.

"**On behalf of the Great Octopussy Anarchic Alliance**," declared the ancient Lovecraftian comedian, "**I, Cthulhu, the Great Crotchety Old Fart of the Depths, do hereby formally accept the Federation's standing offer of membership. With conditions**."

Patrick sighed heavily, looking too exhausted and resigned to argue with the self-styled inventor of fictitious titles. "And what are the conditions?" he wearily asked.

"**I command that you change the name of the planet back to Varuna**," the Great Crotchety Old Fart of the Depths demanded of the Governor. "**The Wigglebiggle joke has grown old**."

Patrick's face... twitched. Even through his exhaustion,

Lisa caught a momentary glimpse of his feelings, enough to guess as to what he must be thinking at that moment. It most likely involved deep sea fishing. *With explosives.*

The others present had begun to bicker with each other, a dozen *sotto* voiced arguments and discussions going on around the table. Chun was rubbing Patrick's shoulders comfortingly, and giving Lisa an amused grin over the top of his head.

And Lisa – who had achieved what she had been commissioned to do, and who was mercifully exempt from dealing with the aftermath – turned and walked away. She felt giddy. And amused. And deeply, deeply proud and satisfied with herself. But most of all, she felt exhausted, and her head was pounding, and she needed to get out of her armor and lay down in private.

But as she walked away, a sudden realization came to her. *I was right all along. It really **was** all just a joke.*

Chapter 28

Deep breaths.

The job was finished. Payment had already been transferred. The tasks at hand were the province of Governor Patrick Chu and his fellow administrators of the former-and-once-again Varuna. Lisa was free to do as she pleased, until such time as another client required her services. She could have spent the next few weeks pigging out in the privacy of her assigned quarters – or simply stayed aboard the *Hearth*. She could have retreated into comforting solitude with books and video games and with thick physical barriers between her and the people she had forced herself to interact with, at the cost of considerable stress and anxiety.

But Lisa had spent too much of her life allowing the wounds of the past to deny her present opportunities for happiness. She was breathing deeply, deliberately, fighting to control her heart rate, as she prepared to open the door and emerge into the hall. *Deep breaths. No one is counting on you. No one is relying on you. You can enjoy yourself without worrying.*

Lisa continued to tell herself such deliberate affirmations, as an aegis against the terrifying uncertainty of social interactions. Then she opened the door, and froze at the sight of the off-duty Chief Jingcha before her.

The uniforms worn by the Jingcha were fairly standard. The tunic was thick, offering limited protection against abrasions, cuts, and of course the cold. It also provided a naturally neutering effect upon the wearer's physique, establishing that here was an officer of the law, sexless and *uniform*. By contrast, Chun's cable knit sweater was looser and at least as bulky, yet somehow it emphasized her femininity. Perhaps it was the loose, flowing skirt that accompanied it. *Or maybe it's...?* No. Surely she hadn't.

She had. Lisa had no grasp of cosmetics. Her face had always been something to conceal behind her helmet, not to adorn with makeup. But Chun had done things to her lips and cheeks and eyes, and somehow it made her indescribably alluring – while still being unmistakably *Chun*. She was a new Chun, a magnificent Chun, but still definitely a Chun.

A Chun who was silently mouthing something in either Gaelic or Mandarin, her eyes wide as saucers as she took in Lisa's own appearance. Lisa felt her cheeks flush under the scrutiny, and she was already second guessing her dearest Jenny.

She'd handled all the correspondence through Jenny, feeling more comfortable asking another woman about such delicate matters. Jenny had provided emphatic and soothing reassurances that Lisa was free to have sex with anyone she pleased. Then she had relayed an additional message about how, if Lisa's new friend ever wished to come visit Furcadia, a certain lapine royal servitor would be delighted to commit some "crimes of passion" against an officer of the law. After some hyperventilation and lurid fantasizing, Lisa had managed to shoot back a retort about hoping that Brutus would enjoy a bit of police scrutiny, before quickly moving on to the next question of importance. Namely, what to wear for her first date. Her new dress and arm sleeves were striking, but Lisa felt... uncomfortable, wearing them in public.

Jenny had once again proven how wonderful she was, as she intuitively provided reassurance that Lisa shouldn't feel pressured to wear anything she was uncomfortable wearing, or being seen to be wearing. But the vivacious vixen had taken the liberty of looking into Varuna fashions, and had provided a few suggestions based on what she knew Lisa kept in her own wardrobe selection.

Not that it was surprising. Jenny had helped pick out much of Lisa's clothing, after the Huntress had lost the majority of her personal possessions as a result of the near destruction of her beloved ship. And naturally Jenny knew exactly which woolen garments Lisa possessed, and now Lisa was wilting under Chun's scrutiny, because Varuna wool tended to be spun into warm sweaters and flowing skirts. Lisa doubted that Chun had ever even seen someone wearing a "virgin killer" style dress before. And while her front was mostly covered, her back (and shoulders, in all their hard muscled glory) were fully exposed, and Lisa felt like throwing on a shawl or six. Or simply shutting the door, crawling into the bed, and hiding under the covers.

But Chun bolstered her almost nonexistence self-confidence with a single additional vocalization. "Wow." The woman's eyes were wide, and her cheeks were flushed under the cosmetics, and Lisa knew she *meant* it. It gave Lisa the confidence to step out into the hall on the flat heels of her knee high boots. And to allow Chun to hold her hand. The left hand, even – because Chun was well aware of which hand was flesh. And that her prosthetic lacked tactile sense. "So, where did you want to go first?" Chun asked, shyly.

Shyly. I'm not the only one feeling this way.

"Well, if you're okay with it..." Lisa trailed off suggestively. Chun arched her brows encouragingly, and Lisa grinned as she continued, "I actually wanted to go talk to those two idiot fishermen that Tako caught."

"Why, you want to brief them on what's happened during their confinement?" Chun asked, teasingly. "Or did you just want to see the look on their faces?"

Lisa's grin widened. "Yes," she purred. "So they're still in lockup? When are they getting released?"

Chun gently tugged at Lisa's hand, leading her towards the Gongating's holding facilities. "We might as well release them now. It's not as if the Octopussies are going to be pressing charges. Still," she sighed, "at least it was a few days not dealing with their drunken shenanigans."

The Gongating's cells were a subtle reminder of the Jingcha's professionalism. The walls were of transparent material, the cots looked clean and comfortable, and only two cells were even occupied. Lisa was less than surprised to see that both men looked far less disheveled, and far more sober, than they had on her previous encounters with them. And clearly they were very, very unhappy about that.

"Good news, boys," Chun sang out to them as the women approached, a saccharine sweet smile on her face. "You're getting released into your boat's custody!"

The one Chun had identified to Lisa as Archie favored them both with a contemptuous sneer, not stirring from his seat on the edge of his cot. "So did the zhà zhāngyú decide not to press charges?" he growled.

"Tsk. Don't say such things about the neighbors," Chun chided. "Especially when they're being so nice to you."

Lisa couldn't help but admire Archie's surprising talent. He appeared to be able to replicate a Gaian's ocular adaptation. Or at least, he was managing to come close. His eyes might not actually be *glowing*, but they were certainly *blazing*. With fury.

"What? Didn't anyone tell you the good news?" Chun teased him. "The Octopussies are joining the Federation!"

This did not elicit a positive response.

"And there should be easements for fishing soon," Chun added.

Archie frowned thoughtfully at that. Then he looked up, and his attention shifted to the taller, larger woman. "So why'd you bring a date to the lockup?" he demanded.

Lisa felt her cheeks color, and she flinched under the unfriendly attention.

Then the other one, the one whose name was Finfan or something like it, chimed in from his cell. "That's the shǎ bī that was hanging off Glackit Patrick's arm," he observed, his gaze roaming over Lisa's body in much the same fashion that Lisa's gaze tended to roam over barbecued meat.

"Oh, you've got a thing for government types, huh?" Arche noted, his eyebrows wiggling suggestively.

Lisa felt her cheeks growing hotter, the blush spreading to her neck and throat. Her vision brightened as her microevolutionary adaptation kicked in, and she knew her eyes must be glowing.

"Nice trick," Archie grunted, sounding decidedly unimpressed. Finfan made a similar vocalization, his gaze continuing to roam over her.

Lisa shut her eyes tightly, her body trembling with humiliation under their scrutiny.

"So why are you bothering us?" Archie demanded, decidedly unsympathetic to her distress.

*Deep breaths. You came here to gloat. You **won**. You can do this.* Lisa inhaled deeply, then exhaled with a forceful huff. "I just..." *Damn it.* She took another breath, then started again.

"I just wanted to let you know that the case has been solved. You're free to go." She opened her eyes to glare directly at Archie's face, trying to meet his gaze in a challenging fashion. "And the Octopussies never actually intended to expel anyone."

Archie didn't even flinch. His head remained craned backwards as he met Lisa's challenging gaze with a glare of his own. In the next cell Finfan was making a grunting bark of disbelieving laughter at her claim. "What, you're telling us that this was... what? Some kind of joke?" Archie growled, his eyes blazing more heatedly than ever.

Lisa's cheeks were beet red, and her eyes were glowing brightly from her terror, but she was breathing deeply and bracing herself to answer. It was simply too perfect a setup, she couldn't allow herself to fail this. "It was all a joke," she declared, in a slow, deliberate tone. "Making you change the planet's name. The fishing. The "ambassador." All of it. It was all just a bunch of practical jokes."

Archie continued to glare, his eyes boring into hers. But his expression faltered around those eyes, the weather-seamed skin surrounding those eyes smoothing as his frown unfurrowed. Finally he averted his gaze, turning to stare at Finfan. The two men gaped at each other for several long seconds, before one of them spoke.

"Respect," Finfan confirmed, speaking for the both of them. The fishermen nodded emphatically in agreement. "Best prank I've ever heard of."

"Their evolutionary development is..." Lisa began, then decided not to bother with the lecture. Clearly neither men was particularly interested in denouements. "Well, let's just say, you can expect plenty more jokes from your neighbors," she finished somewhat lamely.

Archie chewed his lip thoughtfully. Then his rough

features split into a smirk of genuine amusement. "You know? I think I might get along with the slimy buggers after all," he chuckled darkly.

Chun rolled her eyes and grabbed Lisa's hand, pulling her away. "Come on," she entreated. "Let's go get something to eat."

Lisa didn't need much prodding with an offer like that. Behind her, she could hear Finfan directing a question to his friend. "Hey. Do you think Octopussies like whiskey?"

Chapter 29

"Thank you so much!" Lisa declared, in a voice that positively throbbed with sincerely heartfelt gratitude.

"Thank *you* so much!" Jing echoed, her sweet young face split in a beaming smile as she watched the amazonian offworlder snatch up one of the Varuna rolls. One chomp of Lisa's jaws and several inches of protein filled delicacy ceased to exist, torn from the rest of the sandwich as the Huntress chewed with gusto.

A soft smile twisted Chun's lips as she watched Lisa gorge herself, chin resting in her callused hand as she leaned against the kiosk's counter. She seemed to be content simply to watch Lisa eat, though she had ordered a roll for herself. The teenaged girl behind the counter was already preparing the Chief Jingcha's order, moving with alacrity and flair.

"So how long before the fishermen get their easements?" Jing asked, as she set down the singular roll on the counter next to Chun's elbow. It glistened with its creamy dressing over the beautiful flakes of shellfish flesh, and Chun straightened up to grab at the roll with both hands before taking a greedy bite.

"Mfph," Chun replied, then focused on chewing and swallowing the first bite before answering more coherently. "The biologists... mmm, so good." Chun licked her lips, then tried again. "The biologists still need to confirm the safe limit. We don't want to overfish the local populations."

Jing pouted slightly, glancing up at the taller customer's face as if hoping for a different, more appealing answer. "So, how long do you think that'll be?" she asked, aiming the question at the bounty hunter as much as at the head of local law enforcement.

Lisa said nothing, being entirely focused upon polishing off the rest of her first Varuna roll. Chun provided the clarification for the girl. "It shouldn't be more than a few months before the fishing boats can go back on the water again," she said reassuringly.

Jing beamed happily at Chun, then glanced again at the Huntress. Lisa had begun to devour her second roll, blissfully oblivious to the scrutiny. "It looks like you landed a pretty big catch yourself, Auntie Chun," Jing murmured, in a playfully teasing voice.

Chun laughed at that, a hearty guffaw from her diaphragm. Lisa's cheeks flushed beet red, but she kept eating without retort.

Behind Jing the door to the back of the kiosk slid open, and a mane of fiery red hair poked its way into view. "Is everybody enjoying the food?" asked the lanky limbed man, glancing at his patrons with a beaming smile on his freckled face.

"Mphh. Mmhmm!" Lisa murmured appreciatively, as she made her way through her second Varuna roll.

"Daddy! Auntie Chun said the fishing boats will get to go out on the water again in just a couple of months!" Jing declared happily, her face wreathed with joy at the prospect.

"Uh, I didn't say anything definite..." Chun hastily stammered, rushing to correct the girl's inaccurate declaration. But her words were cut off by a bark of local profanity, a profane blend of Gaelic expletives mixed with Mandarin for maximum offensiveness. Jing's father began to clutch at his red hair in dismay.

"I *finally* got the hang of breeding the èmó de lobsters," he groaned in a tone of utter anguish. "And now you're going to ruin me! Again!"

"Daddy..." Jing chided her father, turning to focus her attention on the man and his histrionics.

Lisa felt a tug at her hand, and made no attempt to resist as Chun pulled her away. They left the bickering parent and child behind them, and neither Jing nor her father seemed to notice they no longer had an audience.

"Thanks," Lisa sighed gratefully, her body flooding with relief at being extricated from an uncomfortable social situation.

"Don't mention it," Chun giggled. Then they both became quiet for a time, walking together in companionable silence. Lisa was grateful for this as well, an opportunity to admire the scenery. The architecture. The buildings had an almost organic quality to them. The rounded geodesic domes that had endured for generations, built by the first colonists upon their arrival. Triangular panels of weather resistant polymers, welded together to form durable, stable structures that remained in use even now. Most of the more recent buildings were of a similar construction, the tradition having been established as each new generation sought to continue what they found comforting. Homey.

Finally Chun broke the silence with a question. "So..." she began, trying to keep it casual. "Um, did you speak with your, ah, "Furcadian friends," yet?"

Lisa smiled softly, then glanced away, her nostrils flaring as she took a deep breath. The scent of the ocean filled her nostrils, salty and with a whiff of the assorted chemicals that made it more than just plain water, or even salt water. *Local chemistry. Waste byproducts from plants and animals. And for all we know, the Octopussies could have some kind of cottage industry going on down there, producing whatever it is I'm smelling.*

Finally, Lisa answered. "They're all okay with us having fun together," she began. In her own head she reflected that *more than okay* was perhaps a more fitting description of their response. "But... they did have a few requests..." She trailed off into silence, then let the silence extend until it grew uncomfortable.

Finally, Chun broke the silence. "What requests?" she almost hissed, sounding frustrated and impatient.

The idea that Chun was so *eager* to have her was deeply flattering, buoying her confidence. The notion that Chun was frustrated with Lisa's equivocation was amusing. She was successfully teasing a prospective romantic partner!

I might actually get the hang of this sort of thing. Lisa grinned momentarily, before her euphoric amusement faded. *Someday*.

"Jenny said she'd love it if you visited Furcadia sometime," she confessed at last. "She said she'd love to be a tour guide for you. Especially if we're both there together, so we can all... hang out."

"Oh." Chun frowned faintly, as she digested this information. Then she nodded judiciously. "That sounds like something I might enjoy doing, in the future." She frowned again, as if calculating available time and resources for an interstellar vacation. "So were there any other requests?" she asked, sounding almost distracted, as she contemplated whatever thoughts were preoccupying her.

Lisa couldn't help but grin again. "Harvey asked if you

could bring the shackles," she confided, watching Chun to see her reaction.

Chun did not disappoint. First came a startled grunt, as if the sheer audacity of the proposition had knocked the wind out of her. Her cheeks flushed darker than Lisa's had under the mockery of the imprisoned fishermen. She turned to glare questioningly at Lisa, as if seeking confirmation that Lisa was being serious about the relayed request, or if it were a joke.

Lisa nodded her head, still grinning. It was a serious request from Harvey, and Lisa knew it. And while she didn't dare offer any encouragement on the matter – in either direction – she couldn't help but speculate.

"Well…" Chun mused, still blushing furiously. Lisa bit her lip nervously, suddenly concerned that she might have given offense. She opened her mouth to say something else, then shut it again lest she add to the offense.

"Well.." Chun repeated, tilting her head in consideration. Then her shoulders heaved upwards in a broad shrug. Then they began to bounce up and down, as the woman giggled. Lisa felt her own cheeks color again, even as her lips curved once again in a smile. This time it was a smile of nervous relief.

I didn't offend. And I made her laugh.

Still giggling, Chun reached out and slipped her arm around Lisa's hip. The taller woman gasped, but made no attempt to pull away. Her own thick limb reached out, nervously – almost gingerly – sliding around Chun's shoulders. *This is nice. This is really nice.*

Arms around each other as they walked, Lisa carefully shortened her gait to match Chun's. Together they walked towards the docks, to enjoy the rest of the afternoon together. As they neared the water a tentacle rose up, breaching the surface to wave in a long, slow motion at the pair.

"Look," Chun exclaimed, pointing at the tentacle.

Lisa nodded in acknowledgment. "I see it," she murmured. Then she frowned, as the tentacle dipped into the water to join with two of its mates, lifting something glistening and transparent out of the water. "Is that... some kind of glass?" she blinked.

"It looks like a porthole. I can't imagine where they got it from." Chun grumbled, visibly annoyed at the prospect of petty theft. Or of littering.

The Octopussy raised the potentially pilfered porthole up higher, then carefully slithered two tentacles about the rim, as if creating a frame. The two tentacles twisted about, twirling the circular lens as they fashioned themselves into a straight rod.

Then – and this was the part that made Lisa gasp – the Octopussy lifted its head from the water until one eye was facing directly at them. The porthole was positioned so that the creature could stare directly at them through the lens, its unblinking gaze fixated upon them.

Chun began to laugh, shaking her head incredulously. Lisa gaped, eyes wide with disbelief as the Octopussy continued to mime the act of inspecting them through a magnifying glass.

"You're Sherlock Holmes, all right," Chun continued to laugh. And Lisa couldn't help but join in, laughing helplessly under the teasing of the creature in the water.

"Is that Tako?" Lisa asked. She raised her hand to wave at the Octopussy in a friendly fashion.

"Hell if I know," Chun shrugged. "But you're the most famous human as far as the Octopussies are concerned. At least, this week."

Lisa laughed again, before turning to face Chun. She

didn't dare try for a kiss, but she felt sufficiently bold to pull the shorter woman in for a hug. And – much as Jenny had done – Chun gave a muffled squeak of surprise, before beginning to... burrow. And Lisa very much felt like letting Chun burrow away.

Out in the water, the Octopussy dropped the lens and untangled its tentacles. Then it lifted two limbs up once again, extending them outwards at a near right angle. The outer lengths curled inward, forming a pair of half circles before touching the tips together. On the shore the two air-breathing aliens – overly serious, often quite mystifying, but nonetheless fascinating and lovable – hugged, oblivious to the shorecomber admiring them through the heart shape she'd fashioned.

About the Author

Andrew Miller is the author and creator of the "Michael Williams Lives in Space" series, the "THUMBS UP!" series, as well as multiple other works in the science fiction and fantasy genres.

During the course of his life he has worked with, and interacted with, a broad variety of eclectic subcultures, organizations, and individuals, ranging from armored Stick Jocks of the Society for Creative Anachronism, to custodial engineers equally adept with building microwave cannons and mopping floors, to USMC officers training to defend against time traveling medieval knights.

His likes include animals (especially dogs), video games, martial arts, cuisine, and good books. His dislikes include bullies, hypocrites, and "teachers" more interested in yelling at students and whacking them with sticks than in teaching (that is to say, teachers who are bullying hypocrites).

His birth sign is Aries, he has no idea why that even matters, and if encountered should be considered talkative and gregarious. Your best option is to put food in his mouth and flee while he's distracted.

www.ingramcontent.com/pod-product-compliance
Lightning Source LLC
LaVergne TN
LVHW041704060526
838201LV00043B/562